BORN OF

Elven Blood

Books in the Dragonflight Series

BORN OF Elven Blood

by Kevin J. Anderson and
John Gregory Betancourt

Illustrated by
JOHN HOWE

A Byron Preiss Book

Atheneum Books for Young Readers

BORN OF ELVEN BLOOD
Dragonflight Books

Atheneum Books for Young Readers
An imprint of Simon & Schuster Children's Publishing Division
1230 Avenue of the Americas
New York, NY 10020

Cover painting by John Howe. Cover design by Brad Foltz
Edited by Keith R. A. DeCandido

Special thanks to Jonathan Lanman and Howard Kaplan

The text of this book is set in Garamond #3.
The illustrations were done in Pastel.

First edition
Printed in the United States of America
10 9 8 7 6 5 4 3 2 1
ISBN 0-689-31815-4
Library of Congress Card Catalog Number: 94-71055

To my niece, Trinity,
who already has a little
Magic in her life
—K. J. A.

To Kim—as always,
my inspiration
—J. G. B.

1

Maria was being followed in the night.

She quickened her pace, and the soft footsteps behind her picked up, too—a gentle soft scrape against pavement, a faint splash in a puddle from the rainstorm. She looked around but saw too many shadows. It was still early evening, but the streets were as deserted as at midnight. And dark. Her heart began to race.

Like many streets in west Philadelphia, small stores lined Beechwood Avenue, their windows blocked with graffiti-covered steel shutters. A stranger could be hiding in any of the dark alcoves, watching and waiting for her.

The next time lightning flashed, Maria whirled, hoping to surprise the follower but not knowing what she would do. She couldn't see anyone in the darkness behind her, but she glimpsed plenty of places for a stranger to hide in the slanting rain.

Something skittered between two parked cars, low to the ground and moving fast. Maria jumped. Was it a dog . . . or a man, shifting to watch her? Her large brown eyes narrowed to slits. Her breath misted in the cool air as she studied the deserted sidewalk. A lump grew in her throat.

She wanted to get home as fast as possible. Maybe she should just start running. Her mom was already going to yell at her for being so late after school.

More lightning splashed the avenue. Only a 24-hour laundromat ahead showed any sign of life. Warm yellow light spilled from its open door like an invitation to safety, but Maria saw no one inside—just empty washing machines, like big blind eyes.

She began to walk again, keeping her head high, pretending not to be afraid. With most of the streetlamps smashed or burned out, the buildings on the block looked abandoned. Maria had never been in this part of Philadelphia alone after dark, and she sure never wanted to be again . . . if she made it home at all.

She hurried faster. A cold, heavy rain pattered down, sparkling the air in each lightning flash. Thunder sounded like an avalanche far away. The rain tapped on metal cars with pinging sounds. Red and gold leaves fell from the trees along the avenue, scraping across the pavement with a sound like dry fingernails.

A thin mist snaked across the gutters and sidewalk, winding around her feet like something out of an old horror movie. Maria shivered. She didn't have an umbrella; she'd be soaked before she got home. Right now, though, her main goal was staying alive.

"I'm sixteen years old," she whispered softly, like a promise to herself. "Nobody better mess with *me* if they know what's good for them! I can take care of myself." She drew up her jacket collar and threw back her shoulders, keeping close to buildings to avoid the rain.

Then she heard the soft footsteps start again. Fear cut through her, and her tough act dissolved like mist in the sunshine. It took a huge effort not to glance back—or to run in blind panic.

The TV news programs kept talking about Philadelphia's rising crime rate, the muggings, the kidnappings and shootings, the drug wars. She didn't *want* to find out who was following her. She walked faster, looking for someone, anyone who might protect her.

But the street remained empty—except for the footsteps.

It was all Mrs. Brandeth's fault. Earlier that afternoon, Maria had gone to tryouts for her school's spring play, *Camelot.* It had been wonderful at first. She'd gotten her copy of the script, Mrs. Brandeth had smiled encouragingly, and Maria had announced boldly, "I want to read for the part of Guenevere."

A few chuckles came from the audience and one outright laugh from Jim Martino, but Maria didn't care. So what if she was a little overweight, and a little short, and a little shy, and her hair was kinky and black? Makeup and wardrobe could fix all that. She could wear a beautiful flowing wig. She could lose some weight or wear slimming tights under her costume.

Mrs. Brandeth smiled and said, "I think you'd make a fine Guenevere, Maria. Jim Martino? Please read the scene with her."

Everyone knew Jim was going to play Arthur. With his Tom Cruise good looks and his athletic body, he was a natural for the part. People like him always ended up class president, captain of the football team, and star of the play. Jim could be a bully when he wasn't being condescending, but Maria wasn't going to let him intimidate her. She had vowed that

she would be Guenevere. It would be just like a
fairy tale.

Smirking, Jim strutted on stage and stood facing
her with his script held casually in hand. "Hey, relax,
Maria," he said with too much sincerity for it to be
real.

Mrs. Brandeth said, "Page 34. Begin whenever
you're ready."

Maria turned to the proper page, cleared her throat,
opened her mouth—and froze. Something inside her
locked up tight, like a car stuck in the mud, but her
wheels weren't even spinning. She tried to speak but
couldn't make the words come out. Mrs. Brandeth
watched her, raising her dark caterpillar eyebrows; Jim
Martino heaved an impatient sigh. The words on the
page might have been written in Greek for all Maria
could tell.

The audience of other hopefuls stirred. Someone
cracked bubble gum. Maria felt her face growing hot.

"Maria?" Mrs. Brandeth called.

"I—," Maria began. Suddenly she didn't know
what she was doing there. She was a fool to think she
could appear in *any* play, let alone opposite Jim Martino. She took a step back. "I'm sorry," she muttered.
"Sorry for wasting your time."

She dropped her script and ran to the emergency
exit at the far side of the stage. The door opened onto
the soccer field and she kept running until she
rounded the corner out of sight. She just wanted to
get home and forget about all this!

She heard the emergency door open again. "Maria!"
Mrs. Brandeth called. "Ma-ri-a!"

Maria bit her lip and tried to hold back the tears.
Leaning against the brick wall of the auditorium, she
sank to the ground and tucked her knees under her

chin. Overhead, the clouds looked ready to burst into their own tears.

So much for being in the play, she thought. Now she truly *was* a failure at everything she'd tried. A single tear tried to roll down her cheek, but she brushed it away before it could.

Maria sat there in the gathering shadows for almost an hour as darkness fell, angry at herself for being such a loser. When she finally stood, brushed her jeans off, and started for home, she didn't want to take the trolley. She didn't want to face her mother and have to explain why she'd been crying. Her mother wouldn't understand. Maybe Mom wouldn't even notice.

Bernie, her stepfather, wouldn't remember about the play. With as much as he drank, half the time he didn't know which day of the week it was, let alone what Maria was supposed to be doing. Bernie had laughed when she talked about trying out for the part, and then her baby brother Scotty had started crying, and her mother had started her tired round of complaining, too worn down to do anything but drag herself from minute to minute.

No, Maria had no reason to hurry back from the play tryouts. Half an hour's walk—it was only thirty-six blocks—would let her compose herself again. She looked forward to the time alone.

Alone out on the streets, as rain pattered down and the mist grew heavier . . . as someone stalked her . . . Maria wished she'd taken a trolley instead. She could be sitting down right now, feeling the trolley car jolt and shiver as it clacked along its steel tracks, starting and stopping as it picked up other late passengers. She could be looking safely out the grimy window instead of being stranded out here in the dark and the rain.

She glanced over her shoulder again but saw nobody. With a rush of relief, she saw a trolley heading her way, stopped two blocks back at a red light.

Maria darted forward to stand under the trolley stop sign on the corner and dug in her jeans pocket. She panicked for an instant but then pulled out a little brass trolley token. The rain began to let up, and the mist thinned.

As the trolley started forward, its wheels clacked on the tracks. It was an old wooden car painted bright red. Posters advertising cigarettes, beer, and movies decorated its sides. A kindly looking black man in a dark blue uniform sat behind the wheel. She'd never been so happy to see anyone in her life.

But the trolley clattered right past her stop! Maria stared after it, her mouth open. "Hey!" she shouted. Then she noticed the sign in the rear window: NOT IN SERVICE. As if to underscore her disappointment, the rain pelted down harder than ever.

Maria took a deep breath. A trickle of cold water ran down her cheek, part rain, part fog, part tears. She brushed it away in frustration, plastering a strand of dark hair against her face. Swallowing, she crossed the street and started to jog up the next block. She had to get home!

Suddenly a man stepped out from a doorway, blocking her path. He had matted black hair, desperate eyes, and a hooked nose that dripped rainwater. He probably hadn't shaved in at least a week. His clothing reeked of stale cigarette smoke and something like spoiled meat; his breath stank of whiskey.

"Kid!" he snarled, "give me some money. I don't want to hurt you." Metal glinted in the man's left hand, a wicked-looking kitchen knife pointed at her stomach.

Maria screamed, pushing her lungs to make the sound as loud and long as she could, as she had been taught in school—never go along with an attacker, make as much noise as you can, attract as much attention as possible—then run for your life.

Her scream startled the man. He staggered backward, and before he could think of anything else to do, Maria fled up a side alley with all the speed she could manage. "Help!" she yelled. "Somebody help me!"

"Hey!" the man shouted. "Come back here!"

The mist around her grew dense, so thick Maria couldn't see to the end of the street. She plunged into the fog, hoping to hide from the mugger.

After another hundred feet, she slowed to a staggering walk, straining to hear, trying to slow her ragged breathing and pounding heart. Heavy footsteps thundered on the sidewalk behind her. The man was still following her.

Maria managed to run again. Ahead, the few working streetlamps cast murky cones of light through the mist. Beneath one, Maria spotted a man walking a small dog. She ran toward him, yelling, "Help me!"

Maria heard a muffled curse behind her and a splash as the mugger slipped. She kept going, wishing she had spent some time training for the track team instead of reading books and fantasizing about the school play.

Ahead, the man with the dog paused to look at her. He was tall and young, about her own age, with long blond hair tied behind his head in a ponytail. He shifted the dog's thin leash to his left hand and motioned for Maria to hurry. His face wore a faint smile of anticipation. "This way!" he called.

Behind Maria the footsteps paused, then she heard the quiet metallic *tchic* of a switchblade. Maria shuddered—a strange flat taste in her mouth and a lump the size of New Jersey in her throat—but she didn't dare look back.

She reached the glow from the streetlamp and grabbed the pole as she trembled all over. She gasped, "Keep him away from me!"

The young man smiled down at her. The mist and drizzle didn't seem to bother him at all. He wore a white shirt with fine ruffles on the sleeves and chest, as though he had just come from a fancy dinner party. His black pants, tight around the hips, flared a bit at the knees, then tucked into black and shiny new boots. If she hadn't been so desperate, Maria might have thought him comical, like some character out of an old movie, an English pirate or French nobleman.

"You ask for help?" the young man asked. His voice held a trace of an accent, vaguely European perhaps, but not like any she had ever heard before in the ethnic neighborhoods around Philadelphia. "Please, do not be concerned. Allow me to take care of everything." Perhaps it was a trick of the lamplight, but when he cocked his head to glance down at her, Maria could have sworn his ears looked pointed.

The mugger hesitated outside of the circle of lamplight, his breath as ragged as Maria's own. She could hear squishing footsteps as he circled them.

The mists continued to thicken, becoming a heavy fog unlike anything she'd ever seen in Philadelphia, the sort of fog she associated with old movies about Jack the Ripper's London.

Maria glimpsed movement to the left: a drifting

shadow, a phantom-shape that appeared, then vanished into the swirling gray. Were there two muggers? A whole gang? Tension coiled around her heart. "Where is he?" she whispered.

"Watching us," the young man said. "He is trying to decide whether or not to attack the three of us."

Maria glanced down at his little dog, not that such a scrawny animal could be much help to anyone. It looked like a mutt, dirty brown and too small to hurt anything. He wasn't even barking.

The squishy footsteps paused. Through the fog she heard a muffled cough; then, more distinctly, the footsteps moved to the left. "Why won't you leave us alone?" she shouted.

Suddenly the little dog started to bark, straining at the end of its golden leash. The young man smiled at it. Maria saw a flicker of something in his eyes, some trace of inner fire that made her uneasy.

Then the mugger lunged toward them, holding the kitchen knife out like a sword in one hand, a switchblade in the other. His lips had split back in a grimace. "Give me your money," he said in a cold, angry voice. "Both of you." His eyes flicked from Maria to the young man.

"Run!" the young man said to Maria, shoving her toward an alley across the street, an alley she had not noticed before. Mist seemed to pour out of it, flooding the street. "That way!"

Maria took half a dozen steps, then paused to look back. The young man released his hold on the dog. Growling, it lunged forward and, with a leap that seemed impossible for an animal its size, struck the mugger in the chest. Both of them tumbled backward into the fog. The timbre of the dog's growls became deeper, louder, more menacing. In the misty shadows, the dog seemed to grow huge. The mugger cursed, then screamed.

The young blond man turned to Maria. His eyes glowed faintly red. "Run!" he screamed at her. "My dog won't hold him long!"

Maria turned and fled blindly, not looking behind her. As she entered the alley, an unpleasant feeling swept over her. Her skin crawled as if she'd just walked face-first into a spiderweb. A sharp, unpleasant odor like sulfur and ozone filled the air.

An animal howled behind her, then came a sharp *crack* like bones breaking.

"Come!" The young man suddenly appeared beside her. He placed a hand on the small of her back and propelled her forward. "Run for your life!"

The fog grew thicker. The walls on either side of the alley vanished from sight, as did the streetlamps. Maria pushed herself to keep up with the young man's frantic pace.

Gravel crunched underfoot. Startled, Maria tried to figure out what had happened to the pavement. After another few steps, she seemed to be running on dew-slicked grass. A park? In the middle of an alley?

An eerie howl rose behind her, followed by a terrified scream that cut off abruptly.

"Go!" the young man shouted right next to her ear. "And do not look back!"

Maria's lungs burned from the sulfur and ozone stench. Her sides felt as if they were about to split. She put on a desperate burst of speed. She'd never run so fast in her life.

A gigantic tree suddenly loomed up through the fog in front of her. A tree!

Though she tried to stop, Maria ran headlong into its trunk. Her head hit, then everything turned dark.

2

Maria woke up from a bad dream into a good one. Opening her eyes, she found herself in a bedroom that might have been designed for a fairy-tale princess. She lay on a long bed under a lacy canopy with a thick quilt drawn up to her chin. The sheets felt cool and slippery beneath her, like satin. The mattress was packed but comfortable, as if stuffed with finely chopped straw instead of bedsprings. The air smelled of honey and nutmeg.

Maria blinked and sat up. On a wooden table next to the bed burned an orange-yellow candle, filling the room with shifting golden light and a honey scent. Beeswax? she wondered.

Other than the bed and table, the room was scarcely furnished. A tall, narrow wardrobe stood next to an equally narrow door. Long embroidered draperies hung along the walls at regular intervals.

Maria had no idea where she was. At home she shared her cramped bedroom with baby Scotty. His crib sat by the door, and her bed was crammed against the far wall, next to the little desk where she did her homework. Maria had shelves full of beat-up paperbacks and posters of rock stars on the walls. The floor was scuffed old linoleum in a pattern better suited for a kitchen.

The floor here, though, was rough-hewn planking that seemed polished by countless footsteps rather than sanding machines and varnish. This place seemed as far removed from her Philadelphia home as a Scottish castle.

Maria's head began to throb. She touched her sore forehead and felt a cloth bandage. Her fingers came away damp and oily with some sort of soothing, minty-smelling ointment.

Then she remembered the mugger, the young man and his dog, then running headlong into the fog-filled alley with a giant tree in the middle. She'd slammed right into the tree! But all that seemed impossible, a million miles away. How had she gotten *here?* Where was she? What was this place?

Maria pushed aside the quilt and climbed unsteadily to her feet. Someone had dressed her in a loose, white nightgown, made of fabric that looked like coarse cotton but felt like silk. It shifted loosely and comfortably as she moved, as if it were melting against her skin. Looking for her jeans and sweatshirt, she pulled open the wardrobe door. A sharp and spicy smell poured out, like the cedar-chip potpourri her mother bought. The pegs inside the wardrobe were all empty.

Needing more than the candlelight to see by, she went to pull open the narrow curtains—but realized they were intricate tapestries, not drapes. Behind them, the walls were cool, whitewashed plaster. The room had no windows at all.

Gingerly, she ran her fingers over the tapestry. It felt brand new. The fine threads looked like colored spider's webs. When she stepped back, she could study the huge pictures woven into it: hunting scenes out of some fantasy novel, with thin, wraithlike people riding winged horses as they fought against lumpy, hulking creatures that emerged from tunnels in the earth.

Maria moved around the room slowly, studying each tapestry. One seemed devoted to a great battle between the elfin people and the lumpy beasts on a great desolate plain. She ran her fingers over it again, fascinated. This was more exciting than starring in *Camelot* any day.

Just as she was about to try the door, it opened on its own. A tall, thin girl about Maria's age stepped inside. She balanced a tray laden with plates of delicious-looking foods.

"Hello," Maria said, her dark eyes focusing on the tray. She hadn't realized how hungry she was. Before tryouts for the play, she had eaten half of a leftover sandwich, but that was all. The mingling aromas— some spicy, some sweet—made her mouth water.

The strange girl smiled at her and crossed to the table next to the bed. She set the tray down, then patted the bed for Maria to sit.

Up close, the girl was strikingly beautiful. She had a narrow face, high cheekbones, full lips, and huge green eyes that sparkled in the candlelight. Her hair hung in a long curly mass the color of cinnamon.

When Maria sat, the girl handed her a small metal plate with two round pastries made of flaky dough dusted with powdered sugar. They smelled wonderful, a little like the baklava she'd once eaten at a Greek street festival.

"Do you have a fork?" Maria asked.

The girl smiled at her again but said nothing. Maria looked at the tray and saw no silverware, so she decided to use her fingers. The little cake was filled with spiced ground meat, and not at all sweet. The insides steamed; the spices showered her mouth and throat with a delicate nutty taste like almonds—but not quite.

When Maria finished, the girl handed her a pewter goblet filled with cold, fresh water that had a lingering fruity taste. Next, she set to work on another plate heaped with thin slices of cold, pale meat. Maria didn't think it came from a chicken . . . a Cornish game hen, perhaps? She'd heard of those but never eaten one. The fowl was delicious, peppery, and a little tart. After that came fillets of broiled fish stuffed with fresh herbs, nuts covered with sticky honey, a few more small pastries, and finally a bowl of water for dipping her fingers and a cloth napkin to wipe them on. Maria couldn't remember ever tasting food so good.

Finally, with her hunger gone, she turned her attention to the strange girl beside her. Maria pointed to the tray. "What was all that?"

The girl gave her a puzzled look. Her mouth moved, but her words sounded like music—strange tones and lilting sounds.

"I don't understand," Maria said. "Do you speak English?"

The girl laughed, a sound like ice tinkling off of winter branches with the first thaw of spring. As she tossed her cinnamon hair, Maria noticed that the tips of her ears ended with delicate points.

The door opened again; a young man stepped through with a thump of boot heels on the wooden floor. Maria recognized the man who had been standing with his dog under the streetlamp—the man who had rescued her.

He looked handsome and dashing in his leather pants and vest, with a white shirt that puffed out at the sleeves. His wavy blond hair was pulled back into a thick ponytail and tied with a leather thong, exposing his own pointy ears.

Before Maria could think of a question to ask him, the young man strode over to the bed. Smiling at her, he dropped down on one knee and took her hand in his own. "Greetings, lady. Welcome to our home. I am Cyn, and this is my sister, Deirdre." He nodded to the cinnamon-haired girl. "I hope you are feeling better now."

"I—I'm Maria Blanca," she stammered, blushing furiously at his formality. "How did I get here? Where are we?" She touched the sore spot on her head. "What happened?"

"You ran into a tree," Cyn said. "I took you home, my sister bandaged you up, and we put you to sleep for the night. How do you feel?"

Maria lowered her eyes, her heart fluttering in her chest like a butterfly's wings. "I'm a little confused." Then she looked up with a start. "I need to call my mother! She'll be frantic, wondering where I am. If you could just let me use your telephone—"

She tried to stand up from the bed, but Cyn put his hand on her shoulder and gently pushed her back down. "Don't trouble yourself, Maria. Your parents will not have missed you. Less time has passed than you think. Rest awhile here. We like to keep our guests comfortable."

"But—"

The girl, Deirdre, said something to her brother in her chiming, wordless voice again, and Cyn nodded. Maria looked from one to the other in confusion.

Noticing the expression on her face, Cyn straightened in surprise. "Oh, a thousand pardons, Maria!" He reached into a pouch at his side and pulled out a golden ring made of seven thin strips of luminous metal braided together. "Here, this will help you understand."

Maria turned it over in her hand, watching how the candlelight flickered on the shining strands. "This is beautiful. What's it for?"

Cyn said, "Certainly not for staring at. Put it on!"

Maria slipped it onto the index finger on her right hand. The ring seemed to adjust itself to fit perfectly, its woven strands drawing tight like a toy Chinese finger trap.

Her hand grew warm, and the warmth surged through her body. Her head pounded. The room spun dizzily, seemed to flip itself around, and a dozen whispering voices filled her head. She pressed her hands to her ears, alarmed. Just as quickly as it had started, though, the disorientation passed.

"Can you understand me now?" Deirdre asked. Her voice still sounded musical, but her words were clear.

"Yes!" Maria said. "What just happened? How did you do that?" She looked down at the golden ring on her finger.

"Magic," Cyn said in a hushed voice, raising his eyebrows as if at some joke.

"What?" Maria could hardly believe what he had said.

"Don't worry," Cyn answered. "You're going to be surprised by a lot of things. Deirdre will help you get dressed. When you're ready, meet me in the common room. We've got a long journey to make, and some important news to bring the king." He gave her a nod, then slipped out the door with startling speed.

"Just a minute!" Maria cried, leaping up. But Cyn ignored her. "I can't go on a journey with you to see some king! My mother must be going crazy with worry about me. I really, really have to get home. What happened to my clothes?"

"I've got plenty of gowns you can wear," Deirdre said.

"I want my own clothes," she asked. "I mean, thanks for helping me and all, but . . . I really have to get back."

"Wait here," Deirdre said. "I'll be right back."

Maria plopped down on the edge of the bed while Deirdre went into the hall. Cyn and his sister had to be playing some kind of joke, and she didn't like it. She'd had enough of that in school to last her a lifetime. No matter how delicious the meal and how comfortable the bed, she couldn't let herself become distracted.

Deirdre returned in a moment with a ruby-pink fairy-tale dress in her arms. Maria stared, speechless, at the most beautiful dress she'd ever seen. The fabric sparkled in the candlelight; tiny white bows at the cuffs, collar, and hem went perfectly with the lace accents. "You want me to wear *that?*" she asked.

"It might look flashy," Deirdre said, "but it's really quite comfortable, even practical. Much more so than the stiff, puffy dresses in your world. I know—I've tried them on. Feel how light this is. I've played lawn games in this gown, hiked through the forest, even ridden horses in it."

Maria closed her right hand, feeling the strange gold ring. Cyn had said it was magic. . . . He'd also mentioned bringing news to a king. That was the sort of stuff fairy tales were made of. Maria hadn't missed Deirdre's comment about clothing "in your world" either. As she looked at the dress and felt the warm ring on her hand, somehow "magic" didn't seem so impossible. If this was make-believe, would it hurt to play the game a little while?

In her own home, Maria always ended up with poorly fitting clothes picked up at thrift stores or handed down by older cousins. Never in her life had she worn something as beautiful as this gown! She felt like Cinderella.

"Try it on," Deirdre said. She raised her eyebrows, holding the gown toward Maria.

"Will it fit me?" Maria asked, suddenly despairing of her own figure. Deirdre was so thin—

"Of course." Deirdre smiled.

It took only a second to slip the dress over her head. Then Maria stood there, looking down at herself, feeling how the dress clung to her as if tailored to her body. The intricate buttons and laces posed a moment's problem, but Deirdre's nimble fingers helped fasten everything properly.

At last Deirdre stood back, and Maria turned around once, feeling the cool fabric rustle against her skin. It flowed with her, allowing her to bend and turn, and it felt light as gauze.

"You look beautiful, Maria," Deirdre said. She helped Maria quickly brush her hair and wash her face. "Now let's go find my brother."

Together they left the room and went into a long hallway with dozens of doors opening to either side. The hallway ended in a broad stairway.

"Where are we?" Maria asked.

"It's a small inn called the Gold Gryphon," Deirdre said. "My brother and I always stay here after journeying to your world. It's close to the Doorway."

As they descended to a bustling common room full of tables and benches, Maria stared. Dozens of handsome men and beautiful women dressed in flowing

clothes sat eating food, drinking from tankards, talking and laughing. They all had Cyn and Deirdre's
pale skin, delicate features, and pointed ears.

A broad stone fireplace with a snapping fire filled
the back wall. Pots on long metal arms hung close to
the embers. Filling another wall was a wooden bar
whose front panels were carved with scenes of wonder
and adventure similar to the ones in the tapestries.
Colored glass bottles filled the shelves behind the bar.
The windows on one wall let a flood of bright sunlight
into the room. Outside, Maria could see a large yard
of trampled earth, and beyond that rolling green fields
dotted with clumps of red-leafed trees and distant
cottages.

Maria swallowed. "I'm not in Philadelphia any
more, am I, Deirdre?"

"No," Deirdre said. "Faery is a place of many
wonders."

Faery? Maria gasped at her. The mythical land of
enchantment where magic worked. She had read
plenty of bedtime stories about Faery, and her grand-
mother used to leave saucers of milk on her back step
at night for "the wee folk," but Maria had never be-
lieved in it. Magical lands seemed impossible, like
a dream you wished would come true but knew it
never would.

"Cyn must be outside," Deirdre said. "Come on,
we'll have a drink while we wait for him."

Maria started to say she wasn't allowed to drink,
but she followed her new friend to an empty table.
Deirdre waved to one of the women waiting on tables.
The woman came to their table with two tankards of
delicious spiced apple cider.

As she continued to look around with amazement,
Maria noticed a group of older people pulling their

tables and chairs together near the fireplace. "What are they doing?" she asked.

"They're going to tell stories," Deirdre said over the rim of her tankard.

Maria gazed with new interest. Most of the tavern seemed to be quieting down and giving them full attention.

"I've heard them a thousand times before, but you'll probably enjoy them," Deirdre whispered. "Storytelling after meals is a custom here. Cyn says that's all they ever do."

One of the old men took a sip from his tankard and gave a contented sigh. "Yes sir," he said loudly. "Them was the days."

"True enough." A potbellied man with a patchy beard leaned forward. "Did I ever tell about the time me and Old Farrel came across a surviving trog out in the forests to the northeast of here? One-armed, the trog was, and in that arm he carried a spiked ball and chain!"

"Aww, not again, Taber!" One of the old men snorted and waved his hand in dismissal. Several of the others also groaned. "You've told us that one a dozen times over! And it happened years ago!"

This seemed to annoy Taber. He sat stiffly in his chair. "And when's the last time anything interesting happened to *you*, Morven? Tell me that! Since nobody else here has had any better adventures in recent memory, *I'm* going to tell my story about the one-armed trog!"

"Suits me," someone else mumbled, joined by a general murmur of agreement.

The tavern's front door creaked open, letting in a cool autumn breeze. Cyn stood there wearing a redlined black cape over his shoulders. He raised a ser-

pentine riding crop in his right hand, waving to Deirdre and Maria, then strode into the inn. He let the
door slam behind him.

"Ready to go?" he asked. "The carriage is waiting."

"Here now, Cyn," Taber called. "We was just about
to start the stories."

Cyn started. "Let me know when you have a new
one," he said. "I've heard everything everyone has ever
done fifty times by now."

"But your new friend hasn't heard, have you,
missy?" He looked right at Maria.

"I—uh—" Maria began.

Cyn took her arm. "They'll have the same stories
at tonight's inn," he said. "The same ones *everywhere.*
We have to go. The king has to be warned. The trogs
are active again."

Several of the old men laughed. "Don't you believe
it!" they called with derisive hoots. "We wiped the
last of 'em out three hundred years ago!"

The whole tavern was laughing at Cyn's words by
the time the three of them made it outside. It was
just like her school play, Maria thought, blushing.
She was glad when the door closed and the old men
went back to their worn-out stories.

She breathed deeply, looking around. The day was
crisp and cool, just like early October at home. Above
them, the cloudless sky glowed an azure blue, as perfect as the ocean in summer. The air smelled incredi-
bly clean, with just a trace of wood smoke from the
inn.

Fields rolled for countless miles to the front of the
inn while heavy forest stretched behind. The sun had
just cleared the tops of the trees, setting alight the
fiery red and gold of the leaves. Everything looked

picture perfect, like a scene from *The Hobbit* come to life.

Deirdre headed for a small carriage. It was white, with golden trim and open-air seats covered with what looked like velvet. Two cream-colored horses with ribbons plaited in their blond manes stamped in their harnesses, eager to be off.

Deirdre climbed into the back seat. Cyn helped Maria up, then climbed into the front and took the reins. When he made a clicking noise, the horses tossed their heads and started down the winding dirt road at a trot.

"Here," Deirdre said, pulling a blanket out from under the seat and opening it across their laps. "It's a long trip out in the open."

Maria leaned forward to ask Cyn, "What was that all about, back at the inn?"

He shook his head in disgust. "Everyone has become too complacent. Like those old soldiers, they just sit around listening to the same old stories again and again. It's easier to sit and listen instead of doing something new and exciting."

"Well, I'm certainly excited by all this . . . strangeness," Maria said.

Cyn turned a lopsided smile in her direction. "The excitement's just beginning," he said. "We're going to Metgarde, the city of the elves."

3

E lves?" Maria said. "You mean like *real* elves? You've got to be kidding."

"Don't you like elves?" Deirdre gave her an odd look.

"Like them?" Maria laughed. "I don't exactly *believe* in them." Seeing Deirdre's eyes go wide, she hastily added, "It's just so, well, *confusing*. I don't even know how I got here."

"I know everything is happening quickly for you," Deirdre said. Her voice was soft and soothing, hypnotic. "But don't you like what you've seen so far?"

Maria remembered the beautiful bedroom, the lovely and comfortable gown she had on, and the delicious food she had eaten. With a brief thought of her stepfather Bernie's scowling face, her baby brother's wailing in the middle of the night, her own cramped and disappointing bedroom, she let out a long sigh. "Yes, it's all wonderful, special, and . . . magical. Exactly what I've been looking for as long as I can remember. But that still doesn't *explain* anything."

"We had to help you, Maria," Deirdre said. "Cyn and I were shopping in your world. You called for help. Cyn came."

"Shopping?" Maria said.

"I got a new pair of black boots." Cyn pointed to his feet. "Human-made, nothing but the finest. Deirdre bought bracelets of beautiful colored plastic, and we found some of your strange and delightful little windup toys. The king loves them, you know."

"But what am *I* doing here?" Maria said.

Cyn shrugged. "I only meant to bring you to Faery for a minute, but when you ran through the gateway between worlds, you hit your head. We thought it best to get you bandaged up."

Maria blinked her eyes in confusion. "But why didn't you just call for an ambulance or something?"

Cyn frowned at her. "The Doorway was closing. You can only keep it open so long, you know, and I didn't want to be stuck in your world until somebody from Faery could open another gate. That's very hard to do."

"Besides," Deirdre said, "your forehead was bleeding. You did spend two full days asleep, you know."

"Two days!" Maria cried. "My mother must be—"

"Oh, she won't have missed you yet," Cyn said.

"But I've got to get home—"

"Your home is with me now," Cyn said, his eyes flashing. "*You* asked for help. I granted it. Freely asked, freely given. That's the rule."

"Oh, Cyn! Don't be stuffy." Deirdre turned to Maria. "It won't be so bad here."

"But I've got to go to school, and—"

"There's a difference in time between worlds," Deirdre said in a reassuring tone. "Months here will be only a day back on your Earth. We'll make sure you get back safely. Think of it as a vacation."

Maria thought of her crying baby brother, her tired mother, and drunk stepfather. She recalled her humiliation at the *Camelot* tryouts, and how frightening the mugger had been. Then she remembered the beautiful clothes, the tapestries, the fireside stories of old adventures. Now she was on her way to see the king and a city of elves. Did she really want to go back so soon?

"All right," Maria said. "A *little* vacation would be nice."

As they traveled, the road entered a grove of oaks and the sun began to sink behind the hills. Cyn and Deirdre began to talk about Metgarde and what Maria might expect to see there.

"It's almost time for the harvest festival," Cyn said. "There'll be parades through the streets, parties at night, musicians and dancers and magic tricks. I think it's my favorite holiday of the year."

"The harvest festival is nice," Deirdre said with a happy sigh, "but my favorite is still Ice Night, on the eve of the winter solstice. Everybody in Metgarde carves beautiful ice sculptures, shaping them after heroes from the Trog Wars, and they trade them with friends. The master sculptors work behind cloth walls in the central market for a week getting ready, and at the stroke of midnight, as fireworks light up the sky, their creations are unveiled for everyone to see. Each year they create miniature scenes from the great battles."

"You're not really supposed to use magic to do any of the shaping, but everybody does," Cyn said. "Last year I made a huge sculpture of a gigantic trog. It looked so nasty it almost melted the other sculptures just by being near them!"

"And then," Deirdre continued, "the king gives an award to the best ice sculpture, which is then melted down and the water used for making a very rare and

special type of wine that only the royal family gets
to drink.

"After those festivities, after the fireworks, far into
the night, everybody sits in the cold dressed in their
furs and watches their frozen breath steam upward.
We look at the stars because a meteor shower comes
at the winter solstice every year. We watch the streaks
of light flashing across the sky. Legend has it that
those are arrows from the Trog Wars, shot high, high
up into the heavens and finally, over the centuries,
they're falling down. They burn with the speed of
their fall."

Maria caught her breath. "That sounds wonderful!"

"Now," Deirdre said, "I want to hear more about
that shopping mall in your world. What do you call
it? The Gallery?"

"Hush!" Cyn pulled on the reins to slow the horses.
He looked from side to side into the dense trees
around them. The horses snorted and shifted nervously, ears pricked forward. Their eyes were wide.

Maria noticed how dark and shadowy the forest had
become. With night coming on and the ancient tree
branches arching overhead in a leafy tunnel, the carriage stood in a greenish gloom. They couldn't see
more than ten feet to either side: the road twisted out
of sight ahead.

"What is it?" Deirdre asked softly.

"I heard an odd noise," Cyn said, his voice just as
low. "I think something large moved ahead, in the
shadows by that oak."

Maria stared, straining to see. A faint evening mist
rose from the forest floor, but nothing else moved.
"Are we in danger?" she whispered. With a shudder,
she recalled the mugger stalking her. "Do you have
any weapons?"

"We have our wits," Cyn said. "Let's hope we don't need more than that." He had his eyes half closed, concentrating, as if trying to think of a way out.

Suddenly, with a roar and crash of breaking branches, half a dozen huge lumpy beasts in crude leather armor broke from mounds of dirt beside the road, clawing their way upward and emerging caked with mud. Maria looked back and caught a glimpse of huge, razor-toothed mouths, red eyes, and flared nostrils. Each creature carried a wooden spear with a steel tip; several held spiked clubs. They lumbered toward the carriage.

"Get down!" Cyn cried, whipping the horses.

No sooner had Maria ducked than a hefty spear hurtled over her head. It struck an oak tree near the carriage. She saw the spear shaft quivering faintly.

"Run!" Cyn shouted to the straining horses. "Faster!"

More mud-covered spears flew through the air, whistling overhead. One banged against the side of the carriage without doing any real harm. Another crashed into the thick underbrush at the side of the road. The horses whinnied in terror.

Maria risked another look back. The monsters bellowed behind them. Several heaved moss-covered boulders at them.

Cyn flinched to one side just as a broken rock whistled past his shoulder. It struck the flank of one of the horses, but the horse was so panicked it didn't even notice.

"Hold on!" Deirdre shouted. She grabbed Maria, and they both huddled down. Cyn snapped the reins again and again.

At last the carriage rounded the bend in the road, lurching a bit in old ruts. The left wheels lifted from the ground, but Cyn leaned into the turn, and the carriage righted itself. The horses galloped wildly.

Maria popped her head up to glance back at the road. Four burly shapes staggered after them, falling rapidly behind. Their massive arms, clogged with dirt and more gnarled than driftwood, ended in huge hands with claws like fistfuls of railroad spikes, perfect for tunnelling through dirt. Their flat, ugly faces were mostly lost in the gloom. Maria stared until another turn in the road lost them from view.

Eventually, Cyn eased the horses back to a walk. They still quivered with fear; foam flecked their sweaty backs. They tossed their heads and continued to whinny pitifully.

"What were those things?" Maria gasped.

"Trogs," Deirdre said in a choked voice. Her cinnamon-colored hair hung in tangles, and her eyes were wide and frightened.

"We'll spread the alarm when we get to the next village," Cyn said. "The countryside must be put on alert."

"Then the rumors are true," Deirdre said numbly. "I thought they were just stories, but the trogs really have come back. They weren't all killed in the wars."

"No," Cyn said, "they weren't."

"What is this?" Maria asked. "I don't understand."

"Long ago," Cyn said, "there was a great war between the elves and the trogs. After centuries, neither side was able to gain a decisive victory. Every time we beat them back, they hid deep underground until their numbers swelled, then they crawled out of their buried tunnels and attacked more ferociously than ever. At last, when the country lay in ruins—right up to the gates of Metgarde—the last warrior-king, Eran, led a band of men and elves deep into the tunnels, killing every trog with a deadly fire-magic he summoned from the heart of the world. The trogs were utterly destroyed—or so we thought."

"That was about three hundred years ago," Deirdre said.

Cyn said, a little bitterly, "Everyone wanted peace—and finally we had it. But what a cost! Half of our own people were dead. Fifty thousand acres of our most fertile farmland lay wasted and burned by King Eran's own army. More had been destroyed by the trogs. We could barely feed those who survived the war. Slowly, though, everything returned to normal."

"Until now," Maria said.

Cyn nodded. "The surviving elves fell into a lethargic and peaceful existence. The trogs were our greatest enemies, and they had been vanquished. We've had three centuries without war or strife. Perhaps it was too good to last."

Deirdre nodded and clutched Maria's arm. "But the trogs may not be alone this time. A renegade elf named Mask is supposed to be helping the trogs. He formed some kind of unholy alliance with them. I'd considered it just another rumor, but now. . . ."

Cyn snapped the reins. "Yes, it must be true, all too true."

"You said there hasn't been any war in three hundred years," Maria said, "but those old soldiers at the inn. . . ."

"Elves live a long time," Deirdre said.

Cyn urged the horses to a trot again. They began to make good progress through the darkening forest. Full night couldn't be more than an hour away. Cyn kept a sharp lookout this time, concentrating hard on everything around them.

"How far is the next town?" Maria asked.

"It's around the next bend," Cyn said tersely. "We can have a good meal, sit around the common room fire, and tell of the adventures we've had today. There should be plenty of willing ears for a story about something *new*."

The trees grew shorter and farther apart as the road curved into hillier ground. But as soon as the trees receded, Maria spotted tendrils of black smoke drifting into a dusk-colored sky.

Cyn had spotted it, too. "Something's wrong," he said, slowing the horses to a walk.

As the village came into view, the horror became apparent to Maria. Dozens of small dwellings had been burned to the ground, leaving mortared-stone fireplaces standing like lonely sentinels in the twilight. Other houses had been smashed, the walls battered down and broken by hurled boulders. Maria saw only blank, staring holes where windows had once been. Huge shafts opened in the soft ground from which trog attackers had emerged.

The ashes of the village still smoldered. An oily black smoke drifted toward the sky and across the ground half hiding an even more grisly slight. Dozens of bodies lay where they had fallen like so many rag dolls. Men, women, even a few children, all brutally murdered.

Maria swallowed and had to look away.

"Oh no," Deirdre whispered. "Oh no!"

On the other side of the village lay the site of a horrendous battle. Dozens of elves lay motionless, face down in the dirt, each clutching a sword, a knife, or a bow. They had fought bravely, but in vain.

Maria spotted three dead trogs against broken tree

trunks, like pincushions with dozens of arrows sticking out of them.

Cyn brought the horses to a halt and stared wide-eyed at the wreckage.

Tears rolled down Deirdre's cheeks. "We're too late to warn them," she whispered. "We're too late."

4

Let's get out of here," Cyn said grimly, looking at the carnage. "There may still be trogs in the area." He slapped the reins across the horses' backs.

Maria felt sick to her stomach. She'd never seen anything so awful in her life. All those elves lying there torn to pieces. Innocent men, women, and children . . . all the butchered animals and burned houses. In history class she'd seen documentaries about the Nazis and the Holocaust, but this wasn't a grainy black-and-white photograph. These were real people cut down like beasts in a slaughterhouse. She squeezed her dark eyes shut: this horror was as great as all the wonders she'd seen so far in Faery.

As the horses galloped into the gathering darkness, the wan moonlight proved enough for Cyn's sharp eyes to keep the carriage on the road. An uneasy silence fell, with Cyn and Deirdre lost in their own thoughts, and Maria afraid to speak to them.

Just as Maria thought they might never reach safety, they rounded a copse of trees, and several buildings came into view. Windows in the huge, rambling gold mansion blazed with light.

"We should be safe here at the Silver Chalice," Cyn

said, halting the horses. "We're twenty miles from Abraugh Village."

Cyn leaped down from the carriage. Stretching, Maria realized how tense and tired she was. Cyn pulled a loaded trunk from under the seat and lugged it to the door. "Go ahead in," he said, putting the trunk down. "I'll take care of the horses and join you."

"We'll wait," Deirdre said firmly. "I want you to be the one to tell them about the trogs."

After Maria and Deirdre jumped down, Cyn took the harness and led the horses and carriage toward one of the outbuildings. A boy came running to meet him and took the reins. Cyn jogged over to rejoin them. "Now, let's see what we can do inside," he said. He picked up the trunk, nudged the door with his black boot, and ushered Deirdre and Maria in ahead of him.

The Silver Chalice's large common room looked familiar to Maria: sawdust on the floor, white plaster walls, long wooden bar, a high ceiling lined with sturdy oak beams, a staircase in the corner.

Several dozen men and women—elves, Maria saw—had gathered their chairs in a semicircle around the broad stone hearth to tell stories. Everyone fell silent when they entered, though, and gazed at the newcomers with vague interest.

Cyn set the trunk by the stairs and turned to the audience. He said without preamble, "Abraugh Village has been destroyed by trogs. Every last person slaughtered."

Several people in the crowd gasped. "Can't be!" a grizzled old elf called.

"It *was* the trogs," Deirdre said with a little shiver. "They're back again."

"You saw it?" the shriveled old elf demanded, his small bright eyes studying their faces.

Cyn stared at the wrinkled elf. "Old Lawton, you've told more stories about the Trog Wars than anyone else in the land. You remember the carnage. You remember how it was."

Maria said, "They almost got *us*!"

"The trogs attacked us between Abraugh and the Gold Gryphon," Cyn continued. "They dug tunnels in the dirt beside the road and ambushed us as we rode by."

"Aye," said Old Lawton, nodding. "That's trog tactics, all right. I remember my very first campaign— couldn't have been more 'n a lad of thirty or so—we was set upon by a whole *legion* of trogs. Just like that. They boiled out of the woods and tried to take the road, but we held 'em! Blast if we didn't. One elf next to me took a trog spear right in the collarbone, he did, and he just kept right on—"

"Like me and Perrin," another old man piped up. "I remember when the trogs tried to take the road south of Cornace while we were marching past. We held 'em there, too."

"Them were the good old days. . . . " Old Lawton said, a faraway look in his eyes.

"That doesn't help us much now," Cyn said. A note of anger creeping into his voice. "What if they come here? The trogs could be tunneling under the Silver Chalice tonight, right now! We need to set up watches and keep a patrol out. The windows have to be shuttered so they don't notice our lights. And no singing or dancing, so they can't feel the vibrations through the ground. We've got to get ready for them!"

Old Lawton sank back down in his seat wearing an

expression of vague indifference. Everyone else remained silent. Maria looked from elf to elf and saw not anger but a kind of distant apathy, as though not one of them could muster the strength or will to act.

Cyn strode forward as if he wanted to shake them by their collars. "Several of you served in the Trog Wars. Do you still have your swords?"

"Somewhere, I suppose," murmured one. Then another and another nodded.

"Get them!" Cyn said. "If we're attacked tonight, we'll need weapons. Hurry!"

Half a dozen of the oldest elves rose slowly, grudgingly. Four headed for the stairs to the upper floors of the inn and two tottered around Cyn on their way to the front door.

"Does anyone else have a sword?" Cyn demanded.

"Well . . . I have my father's," one middle-aged elf said. Several other elves murmured.

"Get them—and warn your families and friends to stay indoors tonight and listen for digging," Cyn said. "Meet back here in an hour. We'll set up a night watch to patrol the grounds, with a new shift coming on duty every three hours."

"Aye," everyone muttered, but several looked distinctly unhappy at the thought. Cyn shook his head in frustration as he joined them. Maria understood exactly how he felt. It seemed like the elves didn't want to defend themselves—didn't want to leave the warmth and comfort of their little circle by the fire.

Cyn called to the innkeeper for food as Deirdre picked a table near the bar. Maria sat next to her and leaned forward. "What's wrong with them?" she asked.

Cyn shook his head. "We've been at peace too long. The whole country is like this. Everyone is happy and comfortable. Why work hard when there's plenty to eat and drink? Why leave the fire at night when it's so comfortable where you are? Fah!" he sneered. "Three hundred years ago, every man and woman in this inn would have been up and running to get ready for battle! Now look at them."

"Don't they care what happens?" Maria asked.

Cyn said, "Of course they *care*, but it's hard for them to show it. We elves aren't like you humans. We have different problems. We've always been prone to lethargy, letting our sense of duty slide away so we can spend our time at feasts and celebrations. That's why every single week has at least one holiday. In the past we had great causes to rally us, to make our blood boil and our skin itch with the need for action.

"First it was the harpies, who plagued us for centuries. Our king ten generations back destroyed them utterly; for two generations there was peace. Next came the trogs, who bred out of control in their mountain caves, then came pouring out to destroy all we had built. The Trog Wars lasted almost a thousand years and ended only when the old king destroyed *them* utterly.

"Now for the first time in anyone's memory our whole world knows nothing but peace . . . and the elves are becoming lethargic and remote. *Ennui*, I believe it's called in your world."

"It's even worse in Metgarde and the other cities," Deirdre said. "Only the king's orders keep the city running at all."

"I had thought our news about the trogs would rouse the people here," Cyn said. He shook his head. "Perhaps it's too late. Perhaps nothing can save us now."

"Don't talk like that," Maria said. "There's always hope."

Cyn met her gaze. "Not always," he said evenly.

An elf girl who looked about Maria's age carried a tray laden with food. As she set plate after plate of delicacies onto the table, the girl whispered, "Is it true? Are the trogs back?"

Deirdre said, "They confronted us on the road. We were lucky to get away."

"Thank goodness you escaped!" the girl said. "I'm Grania. My brother Corwen and I want to help with the night watch. Someone has to watch out for us! We'll get our hunting bows and be out to join you." Grania headed back for the inn's kitchen without a backward glance.

"She doesn't seem very lethargic," Maria said.

"Maybe there is still hope," Cyn answered.

By then the old soldiers had begun to return one by one with their swords. The blades should have been bright and shiny, but they looked old and tarnished, as if they hadn't been taken out of trunks or off of walls in years. The soldiers headed back to the circle by the fireplace.

Cyn stuffed a bit of bread into his mouth. He dipped his fingers into a rinsing bowl, then rose and hurried over to the soldiers. He maneuvered himself between the old men and their accustomed seats where they had been about to sit down again!

Complimenting them on their weapons, Cyn got them going through a few of their old paces. The routine seemed to be coming back to them. They snapped through several sharp sword-twirls when Cyn called, "Present arms!" The other elves seated around the fire clapped politely, then with more enthusiasm.

Cyn's energy seemed contagious. When Grania and

her brother Corwen appeared from the back room with hunting bows strung and quivers of arrows on their backs, the group began to look like a proper military expedition.

"Your name is Vardon, isn't it?" Cyn asked one of the old soldiers, who nodded. "You'll be in charge of the first patrol."

Vardon stuck his chest out with pride.

"I'll take the second out as soon as your shift is up," Cyn continued. "Go with Grania, Corwen, and this sturdy fellow here." He clapped another old soldier on the back, and the elf grinned up at him. "Old Lawton can take the third patrol. That should bring us to dawn."

"Right!" they all cried.

"Company, form up!" Vardon called. His gaze fell on Corwen as his three charges fell in. "Stick out your chest and suck in that belly, young man! Eyes front, Perrin! Look sharp, Grania! Let's go!" He strode to the door, flung it open, and stalked out into the night, the other members of the patrol at his heels.

Grinning with relief, Cyn jogged back to the table and slid into his seat. "Maybe it won't be so hard," he told Deirdre. "Just give them something to do, and they'll do it."

His sister shook her head. "It won't last," she said. "You got them whipped up for the moment. But next week they'll all be asleep again."

After dinner, Deirdre paid for three rooms with silver coins from a pouch at her belt. Cyn started for the staircase. "Wake me when the patrol comes back," he said to the innkeeper.

With a full stomach and a patrol on guard, Maria found herself growing sleepy. She followed Cyn and

Deirdre up two flights of stairs to the third floor, where they had adjoining rooms. Cyn put the trunk in the middle room, which was to be Deirdre's, then left the two girls there.

Deirdre opened the trunk and pulled out a delicate green nightgown with tiny dancing figures stitched across the hem. "Try this one tonight. It's my favorite."

"It's beautiful!!" Maria drew her fingers across the cloth. Like the dress she now wore, it felt light as gauze. "What's it made of?"

"Fairycloth," Deirdre said. "I made it myself. It's my talent." At Maria's puzzled look, she went on, "My special magic—what makes me different from everyone else. I'm a spinner."

"What's a spinner?"

"Watch." Deirdre dug under the other dresses in the trunk and pulled out a small glass box filled with pins and needles and spools of bright thread. She selected two spools of white, one spool of red, and three needles, which she threaded. Deirdre closed the trunk, put the threaded needles on top, and sat down on the bed with her eyes closed.

Maria watched as the needles rose magically off the top of the trunk. They began to rotate, twisting the thread more and more tightly, dancing through the air. Suddenly they began to duck and weave, dancing together, in and out, out and in, in a blur of movement too fast for the eye to follow.

Maria gasped as shimmering cloth began to appear in midair, just hanging there like a bird on a wire. The needles pulled more thread from their large spools, dipping back and forth, changing colors so swiftly Maria could not see how it was done. A picture started to form on the cloth—

Maria laughed. It was her face, done in such detail it might have been a photograph. The broad lines of her cheeks, the glint in her eyes, the curl of her dark hair—it was all there.

The magic stopped when the picture was complete. Spools, cloth, and needles sank down onto the trunk when Deirdre opened her eyes.

"I'm not a very powerful magician, I'm afraid," she said with a sigh. "All I can do is make things spin around—though I've managed to turn it into a useful talent."

"I've never seen anything like that before!" Maria said. "How wonderful!"

Deirdre smiled up at her, putting the needles and thread back into her glass box. "Keep this as a gift." She handed the cloth to Maria, who ran her fingers over its softness.

"It's beautiful," Maria said. "Thank you."

In her room, Maria slept fitfully. She kept waking, certain she'd heard strange noises outside. Each time, though, it turned out to be a false alarm. Finally she just sat up and stretched the kinks from her back and neck. The air in the room was cool, and a breeze fluttered the curtains. Rising, she padded to the small window and peered out.

The moon had set, but the stars gleamed bright overhead—millions of them—more than she'd ever seen before. They filled the sky like a splash of diamonds on black velvet. The cultivated fields in front of the Silver Chalice stretched as far as she could see. Wind stirred the night-silvered grasses.

She watched for anything remotely resembling the trogs but saw nothing out of the ordinary. Nor, she realized with growing alarm, did she see the patrol Cyn had organized to guard the inn.

Maria stared out the window for a long time. Uneasy, she crossed to the wardrobe, removed the dress Deirdre had given her, and slipped it on. The buttons and laces were less unfamiliar this time, and it took only a few minutes to fasten everything properly.

Finishing, she took a deep breath, opened the door to the hall, and slipped out. A single yellow candle burned smokily in a niche near the stairs, but it shed enough light to maneuver by. Maria crept to Deirdre's room and paused. She heard regular breathing inside. Soft snoring came from within Cyn's room. He must have finished his patrol and turned in for the night.

Maria raised her hand to knock on Cyn's door, then hesitated. What if there wasn't a problem? Cyn had already done his two hours of patrolling. He'd been just as tired as everyone else. No, she thought, she'd better let him rest. But clearly she had to take a quick look herself. Maybe the patrol was just slow. She'd go downstairs and find out.

More confident now that she'd decided to act, Maria descended the dark stairs, holding the narrow wooden bannister. A golden glow came from the ground floor, so she descended more easily.

The scene in the common room brought her up short. Old Lawton and the men in his patrol were all seated around the fire, eyes closed, heads back, snoring loudly.

"What do you think you're doing?" she cried. She stomped forward, clapping her hands sharply. "Get up! All of you! Who's watching the grounds?"

The old elves came awake, staring at her with bewildered, bleary eyes. "What's wrong with the grounds?" one of them asked.

"Just what do you think you're doing?" Maria demanded.

"Sleeping, of course!"

Another added, "Don't you know what time it is? Off to bed with you!" He made shooing motions with his hands. The others were already closing their eyes again.

"What about the trogs?" Maria demanded.

Old Lawton squinted up at her. "Wasn't that last year?"

"I think so," said another. "Or maybe the year before."

"You're all daft!" another piped up. "We wiped out the last of the trogs at Cerntorix ages ago!"

And, to Maria's shock, still muttering to themselves, they all closed their eyes and were snoring again a moment later.

5

Maria stood fuming silently. She could have strangled Old Lawton and his friends!

Leaving the elves dozing by the fire, she made a quick circuit of the inn's shuttered windows, gazing between the slats of each to spy any strange movement outside. At last she satisfied herself that the Silver Chalice seemed to be in no immediate danger. The front door had been securely barred, and the night insects still chirped contentedly outside.

It couldn't be long until dawn. She got a drink of water from a pitcher behind the bar, sat at an empty wooden table, and stared into the fire's glowing embers. If the trogs attacked, *she'd* be the one to raise the alarm. If they didn't attack . . . well, at least the inn was safe.

Before long, the innkeeper bustled in from the back room with an armload of wood. He took one look at the patrol asleep around the fire, Maria sitting at the table, and the shuttered windows and door. "Good morning, girl," he said.

"My name's Maria," she said. "Good morning."

"Pleased to meet you," he said. "Call me Seadon—everyone does." He dumped the wood in a bin next to the fireplace, then tossed a couple of split logs onto the fire. "Breakfast won't be ready for another hour, but we have some mulled cider if—"

Seadon turned toward the sound of boots on the stairs. Maria turned to see Cyn bounding down the steps two at a time. "Who's on patrol?" he demanded.

"Nobody," Maria said with a sigh, indicating the elves by the fire. "They've been asleep for at least an hour. I checked outside myself and didn't see any sign of the trogs."

Cyn strode over to Old Lawton, seized him by the front of his shirt, and hauled him to his feet.

"Wha—" the old elf said.

"Soldier!" Cyn thundered, "you were on duty last night and fell asleep at your post!"

"I—uh—" Old Lawton began, mouth hanging open.

Cyn let him drop back into his seat. "If you were still in the elven army, you'd be executed for that. People were depending on you! We all might have been killed. The trogs show no mercy."

"Trogs?" Old Lawton said wonderingly. "They were real, then? I thought I imagined hearing tales of the trogs' return—"

"It's real enough," Cyn said. "It's *all* real!"

Old Lawton screwed up his face in a befuddled expression. "I'm sorry," he managed. "I know that's not enough. I served under your grandfather, and it never would have happened then. Ah, those were the days—"

The other old elves blinked sleep from their eyes and looked just as guilty. None of them would look Cyn in the eye.

"Times have changed," Cyn snapped. "But we have to change with them if our race is going to survive. Trogs attack by daylight as well as night, don't they?"

"Aye," Old Lawton said, looking up, a trace of hope in his creased old face. "That they do."

"Then don't you think you'd better keep an eye out for them?" Cyn asked.

Old Lawton leaped to his feet. His voice quavered as he called to his men. "Out to patrol!" They picked up their swords and hustled for the door.

Cyn nodded approvingly, then joined Maria at the table. "Deirdre is getting dressed," he told her. "She'll be down in a few minutes."

"Do you want to wait for breakfast?" the innkeeper asked.

"No," Cyn said. "We'll take whatever you can pack for us. I'll harness the horses myself." He glanced down at Maria. "We'll be ready to go in ten minutes."

Cyn, Maria, and Deirdre had come a good distance away from the inn. Deirdre drove the carriage this time as they munched on honey-oat cakes and sipped lukewarm cider under a cloudless blue sky. A morning mist curled across the ground, lending a fairy-tale quality to everything around them. Maria found it easy to put aside the frights of the previous day.

Suddenly Cyn sat bolt upright in the backseat. "Look!" he cried, pointing with his index finger. Deirdre reined in the horses. Maria barely managed to catch herself before spilling her drink.

Maria followed Cyn's pointing finger. In the soft earth beside the track, something had made large, deep gouges . . . *footprints.* Something huge had been walking there.

Cyn swung over the side of the carriage and bent down to the footprints, studying them. "Several days old," he announced. "Probably a trog scouting party from the band that destroyed Abraugh Village."

Maria stood up in the carriage, scanning the fields around them. The day had suddenly taken on an ominous quality. She couldn't hear birds anymore. "There aren't any trogs out there now, are there?" she asked, a cold fear beginning to coil through her stomach.

"I don't think so," Cyn said. He climbed back into the carriage. "But let's get as far away as we can. No place in Faery is going to be safe until the trogs are dealt with."

Deirdre snapped the reins, and the horses launched forward at a gallop. The fields rolled ahead of them, endless miles of tall green-gold grasses, small copses of trees, and the occasional outcropping of weathered, lichen-spattered gray stone.

"It's so . . . empty out here," Maria said.

"We should reach Metgarde tomorrow," Deirdre said.

"That's right," Cyn called over his shoulder. "The capital of Faery. Nearly twenty thousand people live there."

"That's all?"

"Faery isn't like your world," Cyn said with a little smile. "Our people are spread throughout the country, each family tending its own lands. They get together at inns and taverns each night to socialize—what your people would call the 'club scene,' I believe. Twenty thousand is a lot of elves in one place."

When the sun was directly overhead, the road crossed a small stream. "It's lunch time. Let's take a rest," Deirdre said, pulling the carriage over. "I think we must have bumped into a trog scouting party yesterday, a small force to look around and test our defenses. There probably won't be an organized attack for some time . . . perhaps not even till spring."

Maria pulled out one of the carriage's lap blankets

and spread it on the grass next to the stream while Deirdre unhitched the horses. Cyn began to unpack the lunch Seadon had packed for them: spiced meats, crusty brown bread, and another jug of spiced cider. Together, they ate at a leisurely pace.

Maria watched the horses crop grass happily. "It's beautiful here," she said.

"Wait until you see Metgarde," Cyn said.

"Oh!" Maria said. "Wait till you see what Deirdre gave me!" She pulled the square of portrait cloth from her pocket and spread it out. "Isn't it great?"

"Very nice," Cyn said. He smiled at his sister. "You're getting better!"

"I'll never be as good as you are," Deirdre said.

Maria stared at Cyn in surprise. "You're a spinner, too?"

He laughed. "No, I'm a mist-mage."

"He hates when I call him a misty," Deirdre said.

"What does a mist-mage do?" Maria asked.

"Oh, I can shape little creatures from mists," Cyn said. He looked at the creek. "See where that little waterfall is—the spray? Watch."

He closed his eyes, concentrating, and the mist at the foot of the little waterfall began to move. Small figures pulled together out of it, glowing yellow-green like phosphorescent paint. They drifted through the air like tiny ghosts and came to rest above the center of the blanket between Deirdre and Maria. Up close, she could see their tiny faces. "It's us!" Maria gasped.

A carriage pulled by two golden horses appeared, and the figures climbed into it. The miniature Cyn sat in the driver's seat and helped the others on board. Then, with everyone in place, he called silently to the horses, who began to run across the air. The apparition raced around Maria and Deirdre, faster and faster until it became a blur of color. When Maria blinked, it vanished like a burst soap bubble.

Cyn laughed. "Childish tricks," he said.

Maria said, "I've never seen anything like that before!"

Cyn waved a dismissive hand. "It's not that much," he said. "You should see a really big magical working sometime."

"I wish I had a special talent," Maria said. "It looks like such fun . . ."

"Everyone has a magical talent, even humans, even those who first came from your world," Cyn said. "It just takes time to discover it—"

"And time to practice with it," Deirdre finished. "It's taken me years of practice to be a spinner . . . and I'm not that good."

"What sort of talent would I have?" Maria asked.

"It could be anything," Cyn said. "About a third of the elves have talents for spinning, like Deirdre. That's probably the most common. Others can shape fire, water, or mists, like me. That's fairly common. There are some pretty esoteric ones, too. Our mother, for instance, could talk to animals."

"Wow!" Maria said.

"But you're most likely a spinner," Deirdre said.

"How will I know?"

"Do you want to try to find out now?"

"Sure . . . if it's not too much trouble?"

"Not at all," Deirdre assured her. Standing, she moved close to the creek, stooped to pick up a small stone from the bank, and returned to the blanket. She held it out in the palm of her hand. "Look at it, feel it with your mind, then give it a nudge . . . like so!"

The stone began to turn slowly in her hand, spinning like a miniature top. Abruptly she closed her fingers around it, bringing it to a halt. "You try," she said.

Maria took the stone in her hand and stared at it, envisioning it moving, turning first one way and then another. She concentrated harder and harder, picturing it in painstaking detail, how it would move, how it would look as it moved.

But nothing happened.

She sighed and shook her head, dropping her hand. The stone rolled onto the blanket. "I can't even do that right."

Deirdre touched her arm. "It takes time. Besides, if you're not meant to be a spinner, nothing you can do will make a stone move. You have some other talent. We'll help you find it when we get to Metgarde."

"As soon as we take care of business," Cyn said. "We've got to warn the king about the trogs."

They passed two inns that afternoon, and stopped at a third just as night was falling, but the elves there were even less interested in hearing about any new trog threat. The following day proved equally un-eventful. Deirdre and Cyn amused her with tales of life in Metgarde.

"I think the happiest day of my life was when I turned fifteen," Deirdre said. "I'd just made my first complete tapestry with magic and the ladies of the court said the colors would be perfect for the banquet hall and the Feast of the Seasons. I let them hang it up there, though I was afraid it wasn't good enough— that the king and the rest of the men would think it was ugly and didn't belong there."

"What happened?" Maria asked.

"The king came in and said it was the ugliest thing he ever saw," Cyn said with a wicked grin.

Deirdre punched his arm. "The king said it was lovely," she countered, "and everyone agreed with him. What about you, Maria? What was the happiest day of your life?"

"I'm not sure I've had one," Maria said.

"Come on!" Cyn said.

"Well . . ." Maria swallowed. "Maybe my sixth birthday. My father was still alive, and he and Mom had a surprise birthday party for me, with a cake, all my friends, and even a pony. I had such a great time, with so much cake and ice cream I couldn't finish it all, and then riding that pony. The best part was seeing that tattletale Patricia Johnson fall off and get her dress dirty, and everyone laughed at her instead of me. I hoped the day would never end . . . but that was a long time ago."

"Nobody ever had a party just for me," Deirdre said.

"Or me," Cyn said.

As they rode, the landscape changed gradually: low hills gave way to higher ones, grasslands were replaced by orchards and farmed lands with winter wheat just coming ripe. Now and then they passed farms where the people seemed relaxed and complacently happy.

Then they rounded a low hill, and a magnificent walled city came into view. Maria stood up in her seat, transfixed.

It was a city of fantastic designs, of gleaming white spires and gingerbread architecture, of soaring minarets and arching gates, of peaked red roofs and little rooftop gardens. It filled the whole valley, a work of art unparalleled by any human design.

"Metgarde," Deirdre whispered. "At last."

6

As they passed through the elven city's main gates, Maria turned her head to stare this way and that. She could see a series of dragons carved into the gate's stone archway, each with its tail curving around the neck of the one before it to form a chain. Maria wondered if dragons were real in this world.

Seeing her interest, Cyn said, "There haven't been dragons here in two thousand years. Our great-grandmother many times removed killed the last one."

A small, unoccupied lookout tower stood next to the gates, painted in cheery reds, yellows, and pinks. A flower box full of purple blossoms hung below the tower's one window.

"Aren't there any guards?" Maria asked.

"Only at the keep," Deirdre whispered, "and they're just for appearances."

"Do you think we'll have trouble getting in to see the king?"

"Oh, I don't think so," Deirdre answered breezily.

"Didn't I tell you?" Cyn leaned back and gave her a quick grin. "The king is our *father*, Maria!"

"Don't let his fancy talk fool you," Deirdre put in. "He's the king's eleventh son, and I'm the sixth daughter."

"You're kidding!" Maria said in astonishment. "I mean, shouldn't you have bodyguards or something?"

Deirdre gave her a puzzled look. "Who would they protect us from?"

"There's no crime in Faery, no danger, and there hasn't been a swordfight in two hundred years." As Cyn spoke, Maria got the distinct impression that he was disappointed.

The carriage rounded a corner to the edge of a huge square filled with a raucous festival. Colored streamers twined from tall building to tall building, and half a dozen yellow-and-pink dragons made entirely from flower blossoms stood proudly in the center. Brightly dressed dancers with high fluted collars and flared sleeves and skirts swirled to lilting music.

Maria found the musicians seated between the feet of the flower-dragons. A few strummed stringed instruments similar to guitars, but much smaller and more rounded. Others blew pan pipes, and one held a set of miniature gongs on a string, which he struck periodically with a tiny hammer.

Cyn reined the horses in, groaning. "We'll go around. They've started the Festival of the Dragons early this year."

He turned the horses up a side street. Garlands of flowers hung from the windows and crisscrossed the air over their heads. The sweet scent grew as thick as in a perfume store. Each time they came to an intersection, Cyn avoided streets with dancers.

Finally, they reached a wall of solid marble that towered over their heads, topped with pointed parapets. "That's the keep," Deirdre said, "the largest building in the city."

Cyn halted in front of a closed wooden door wide enough to fit the carriage through. He hopped down and strode forward to grab a tasseled gold rope hanging through a slot. A bell jingled somewhere inside. Cyn waited a handful of seconds, tapping his new black boots in impatience, then pulled the bell again.

Finally the door creaked open, and a gnarled old elf peered out. "Eh?" he said. "What do you want?"

"To come in," Cyn said.

The elf squinted at him. "Use the front door."

"There's a dance going on there."

"Then join in the festival!" The old elf tried to shut the door, but Cyn stepped forward and blocked it with his toe.

"Don't you remember me, Buthnot?" Cyn demanded. "I'm one of the princes! Cyn! And here's the Princess Deirdre."

Buthnot squinted at the carriage. "Eh? Cyn? And Deirdre! So it is, bless me! My eyes ain't what they used to be. Why, back in the old days I could spot a trog hidden in the brush from three hundred yards away. Now, that reminds me of a tale—"

"In, please?" Cyn said, pushing the door open.

Buthnot made way for him, still talking about some military expedition against the trogs. Ignoring him, Cyn led the horses forward. Maria and Deirdre ducked their heads as they passed through the doorway. The carriage wheels and the horses' hooves made a sharp, even clatter over the cobblestones. Talking to himself now, Buthnot closed and barred the door behind them.

Maria stared as Cyn guided them through a string of interconnected courtyards. The keep's architecture stunned her. Smiling faces chipped out of stone peered at her from under eaves and odd corners. Slim towers soared to fantastic heights. Windows arched and curled into delicate dragon designs. Lush gardens bloomed in every corner, full of fountains, statues, and little benches where people could sit and pass the time. But as she squinted and looked more closely, Maria thought she saw a general run-down appearance to the place, indications that nobody bothered to take care of the greatness anymore.

Maria could hear music again, and when they rounded a corner, she saw a huge courtyard at the front of the king's keep. Hundreds of dancers moved in intricate patterns before the steps, touching hands, stepping back, stepping forward and around, then twirling away to touch hands with someone else. More musicians played than in the last square, adding flutes, horns, and cymbals.

"There's our father and mother," Deirdre said. "Sitting on the throne at the top of the steps. See? Father's waving to us!" She waved back.

Maria spotted the king. He was a tall, heavy elf dressed in wine-red shirt and pants, with a gold cape across his shoulders and a circlet of gold just visible in his thick brown hair. His face was broad and pleasant, with laugh lines and a rosy glow. He held his head high with a quiet grace.

The king turned and murmured to an elf woman seated on a second throne; they began to clap along to the music. The dancers twirled again as the musicians upped the tempo.

Cyn stopped at a long, low table up against the forty-foot wall. Several young elven boys had been lounging and watching the dancers outside, but they leapt to their feet to take the horses. He climbed down from the carriage and turned to the two girls. "I'm going to see the king," he said.

Before they could say anything, Cyn stalked

through the ranks of dancers. They swirled around him like water around a rock. He didn't look happy.

"Come on," Deirdre said, grabbing Maria's arm. "I don't want to miss this."

They trailed Cyn, cutting through the flow of dancers. Elves twirled around them, wave after wave of bright colors and laughing faces. A handsome elf in a gold shirt with unicorns stitched on the sleeves touched Maria's hand. He beckoned her into the dance.

Maria shook her head. "I can't dance," she said.

"I'll teach you," he promised. "Come on!"

But Deirdre pulled her along, and the handsome dancer vanished into the masses. By the time they reached the steps, Maria was out of breath, but Deirdre didn't give her a moment's rest. They came within five steps of the king, and Deirdre curtsied. Maria followed suit a little awkwardly, self-conscious.

The king paid them no attention. Cyn stood a step below him, explaining in a loud voice to be heard over the noise, "The trogs wiped out Abraugh Village! They slaughtered the inhabitants down to the last man, woman, and child! Mask has gone on the offensive, and we must get ready to strike back. We're all in danger here!" His hand swept the air in a broad gesture.

"A few stray trogs can't be that much of a threat," the king said, craning his neck around Cyn to watch the dancers. "We wiped them out before, we can wipe them out again. Did you bring me any toys back from the world of men?"

"But Father—"

"Tut, tut." The king rose. "I know exactly what we need." The king of the elves held up his hands. Instantly the musicians stopped, and the dancers swirled to a halt. Every head turned in his direction.

"Citizens!" he shouted, and his voice echoed through the square. "Fellow Metgardians! My son has returned with great tales of adventure and romance!"

"But—" Cyn began. The queen shushed him with a gesture.

"Because of the prince's adventures," the king continued, "I hereby proclaim tonight's banquet to be in his honor! Let the festivities continue!"

The elves cheered. Cyn shouted, "That's not what I meant! Listen to me—!" But the musicians had already begun to play again, and all the people took up their dance. "Father!" he cried. "Didn't you hear what I said?"

But the king busied himself talking with the queen. He must have been telling a funny story since both of them burst out laughing. They either hadn't heard Cyn or pretended not to.

The music reached a crescendo. Cyn's words disappeared in a sudden blare of horns. Maria caught something about "fools" and "being sorry," but couldn't quite make sense of it. Cyn stomped up the stairs and through the huge carved doors into the main keep. The doors slammed shut behind him.

"Cyn's always been impulsive," Deirdre said. "We'd better make sure he's all right." She reflexively curtsied to her parents, waited while Maria did the same, and together they rushed up the steps after Cyn.

The doors led into a huge echoing hall. The ceiling arched overhead, and stained glass windows showered them with red, gold, and yellow light. Suits of armor stood on display along the walls; a long red carpet led to a dais upon which sat two enormous stone thrones. They saw no sign of Cyn.

"He's probably upstairs," Deirdre said. She hiked up her skirts and began to climb the stone steps two at a time. Maria was hard-pressed to keep up. On the third floor landing, Deirdre paused to listen. They could hear the distant sounds of merriment from outside, but Maria caught other sounds, too—the clink of metal on metal, low voices talking.

"He must be with his friends," Deirdre said with relief. "They'll calm him down." She swept down the hall, passing rooms to either side and tapestries on the walls.

At the end of the hall she entered a large sunlit room. A round table with carved legs stood in the center, stacked with coins and playing cards. The six young men sitting around it had been playing poker. Only three were elves; the others were humans like Maria. She stared in surprise. She'd begun to think of herself as the only human in Metgarde.

"Well, hello there, Miss!" one of the young men said with a thick southern accent. He was tall and thin, with curly blond hair and a quick smile; he couldn't have been more than seventeen or eighteen. "Whereabouts are you-all from?"

Maria felt herself blush. "Philadelphia."

"Have you seen Cyn?" Deirdre asked impatiently.

"No," the young man answered. "Is he back?"

"We just got in. He had a small argument with our father and stomped off."

He chuckled. "That Cyn is quite a rascal. Aren't you going to introduce me to your friend?"

Deirdre turned. "Maria Blanca, may I introduce you to Charles Andrew Colton. Charlie is one of Cyn's human friends."

"Charmed," Charlie Colton said, coming around the table. He took Maria's hand and kissed it.

Deirdre continued, "These two are my brothers Avaril and Bevan, and next to them is my cousin

Sefton." All three smiled and nodded politely. "Across the table are Felix Grossman and Shane Nutley, both of whom are also from your world."

"Hi," Felix and Shane said. They, too, looked about her age. Felix flashed her a peace sign.

"How do you do," Maria managed to say, flustered and tongue-tied. She curtsied a bit awkwardly.

"If you're looking for Cyn, Miss Deirdre," Charlie said, "why don't you leave Miss Maria here with me? Avaril just cleaned me out on that last hand, and I think I could use a stretch."

"I—uh—don't mind," Maria said. It would be nice to talk to someone from back home. And Charlie Colton seemed polite enough, unlike any of the boys she knew from school. Southern manners, she thought. She'd heard that phrase before, and it certainly fit him.

"I'll see you at dinner then, Maria," Deirdre said, starting for the door.

"Don't you worry, Miss Deirdre," Charlie called after her. "I'll take care of Miss Maria." He scooped up a very small stack of coins from where he'd been sitting, stuffed them into his pocket, and offered Maria his arm. "Miss Maria?"

"Thank you." Maria allowed him to escort her into the hall. Deirdre had already vanished. A couple of drab-clad elves appeared at the far staircase with stacks of fresh sheets. They went into one of the rooms, and Maria could hear them cleaning.

"So, Ma'am, have you seen the gardens?" Charlie asked.

"I haven't really seen anything yet," Maria admitted. "Just some streets and the festival out front."

"Then let's head out back. It's quite something." Turning, he led the way through a maze of corridors to a small staircase. It brought them down to an inner courtyard filled with flowering bushes and trees, pebble walks, a few burbling fountains, and secluded corners with small marble benches.

"It's beautiful," Maria said. The honey-thick scent of flowers filled the air. Hummingbirds, little bigger than her hand, flitted among the trees, their wings a blur of movement.

Charlie paused a few feet down the path and licked his lips. He glanced around nervously.

"What is it?" Maria asked, growing suspicious. Perhaps his manners were too good to be true.

He spoke quickly, "I had to get you alone because I need to ask—begging your pardon, you being a Yankee and all, Miss Maria . . . but do you have any news of the war?"

"The war?" Maria asked. "In the Persian Gulf?"

"Persia?" Charlie swallowed. "No, the war of Northern aggression. You know, the war between the states."

"You mean . . . the Civil War?"

"Is that what you Yanks are calling it now?"

Maria swallowed in sudden dread as she thought she understood. "Charlie . . . what year do you think it is?"

He looked at her strangely. "Eighteen sixty-six, of course."

7

"You're going to find this tough to believe," Maria said, taking a deep breath, "but the Civil War is ancient history."

"Aww, you're not going to start that poppycock, too, are you?" Charlie said. "Shane told me the war ended fifty years before he was born, and darn if he didn't make it sound true. He had all manner of crazy talk about mechanical carriages, and metal vehicles flying through the air. You Yanks are all the same, trying to pull the wool over my eyes!"

"But—" Maria began.

Charlie was shaking his head. "I guess we'll have the same deal as Shane and Felix and I got between us—and that's not to discuss the war."

Maria shook her head in confusion. "If that's the way you want it. But it's true."

Charlie looked up at the sky doubtfully. The sun had disappeared below the walls of the keep. "Would you like to promenade through the garden? We still have an hour before dinner."

"I'd love to. Tell me everything you've done since you've come here."

Charlie shrugged. "Mostly we go sporting in the woods, hunting and fishing, that sort of thing. Cyn's great with a bow, and he's been teaching us, too. I've been showing him tracking, Alabama style. Back home, my folks have quite a bit of land, and I must've tracked, trapped, and hunted every foot of it."

"So, I guess you don't go in for dancing?"

Charlie sneaked a glance at her. "I wouldn't say that, Miss Maria. I reckon I haven't found the right girl yet, is all."

Maria paused to sniff a huge red rose. The heavy scent tickled her nose. A pair of startled humming-birds paused in midair to stare at her before flit-ting off.

They spent the next hour talking in the garden. Charlie Colton was seventeen years old and spent much of his time in Metgarde traipsing through the woods with Cyn. Felix Grossman and Shane Nutley were other Earth recruits of Cyn's: He had brought them to Metgarde over the last year, in the weird time of Faery. The four had been inseparable ever since.

"Have you ever thought about going home?" Maria asked.

"Sometimes," Charlie admitted. "But then I look around, and I know I've never been happier in my life. My mother died when I was six and my father died at Richmond, so there's not much left for me." He paused as a bell chimed somewhere in the keep.

"Dinner," Charlie said. "Would you like to freshen up? Allow me show you to a washroom, Miss Maria." Together they headed for the door.

The banquet in Cyn's honor was even more mag-nificent than Maria could have imagined. Hundreds of tables had been set up with white tablecloths, high-backed wooden chairs, and silver plates, goblets, and utensils. Torches cast a ruddy light over a room that was as large as a football field. Servants moved down the aisles with platters of food and pitchers of drinks.

The king and queen sat at a long table with eight elves on either side. The elves varied in age from children to middle-aged. Cyn sat on his father's right, with Deirdre next to him.

Maria and Charlie seated themselves at a table reserved for special friends of Cyn. Felix and Shane murmured polite greetings to them.

"That's not all of the king's sons and daughters," Charlie said, indicating the elves seated on either side of the king and queen. Cyn kept talking earnestly to his father, but the king paid little attention. "I've never quite gotten the count, but there's at least twenty-three princes and princesses. The queen is some powerful sorceress from the distant land of the marsh elves. She's the shrewd one in the family, or so I hear. I think Cyn and Deirdre got a lot of her in them, too."

Servants brought meat cakes, and Charlie and Maria helped themselves. The food was warm and lightly spiced with nutmeg and something she couldn't place.

A fireball blazed near the king's table as a pair of jugglers performed with burning torches. They tossed the flaming brands into the air as they strolled between the tables. Tumblers and acrobats bounded down the aisles with handsprings and somersaults, building elven pyramids, clowning around. Laughter rang through the room as servants scurried to get out of their way.

"They're wonderful!" Maria said, and Charlie agreed. The acrobats performed through several courses of the meal, and Maria was awed by their feats.

After the acrobats came musicians. Maria welcomed a rest from having to turn to see the performers. Separating into little groups, strolling minstrels wandered among the guests, singing low ballads of past glories.

As plates of honey cakes and fluffy pastries moved from table to table, Maria noticed Cyn whispering something into Deirdre's ear. Nodding, Deirdre rose and headed for Maria's table.

"The king wishes to speak to you," Deirdre said.

"To me?" Maria asked, surprised.

"Don't worry, he only wants to ask you about the village we rode through. The one the trogs destroyed."

"Of course," Maria said. Rising, she followed Deirdre back to the table. She curtsied to the king, looking at the floor.

"Welcome, child," the king said. "You're an honored guest in this house. It's not often we get visitors from your world. You don't have any of those marvelous toys with you by any chance, do you? You wind them up and they walk, or talk, or dance. I have dozens of them in my collection. Marvelous, marvelous little devices. So clever!"

"Afraid not," Maria said, "but I'll find some for you next time I'm home."

"Wonderful!" the king burbled happily.

"About the trogs," Cyn reminded him.

"Nasty creatures. Glad we cleared them out when we did."

"I mean," Cyn said, leaning forward, "the trogs who just destroyed one of your villages. You wanted to talk to Maria about it. Remember?"

"So much bother," the king said.

"Trogs are nasty creatures," the queen said. "Stay away from them."

"Good thing we wiped them out," the king told her, "or there would have been more trouble."

"There's trouble now!" Cyn cried. "They destroyed a village two days ago! They killed dozens of people! Don't you care?"

"Of course I care," rumbled the king. "We can't have trogs doing that sort of thing, can we? Certainly not."

"You wanted to hear Maria's story," Cyn went on. "Tell them, Maria."

Maria swallowed, then told all she'd seen—leaving out only the bit about the old elven soldiers forgetting to patrol the inn. When she got to the part about the murdered village, her voice broke, and she could barely finish.

"They were all dead," she said, her voice a whisper. She looked at the king, then the queen. "It was horrible. I've never seen anything so gruesome."

"So, it's true?" said the queen.

"Every word of it."

The king sat back in his chair, shaking his head. The news seemed a blow to him. "Trogs . . . ," he murmured. "Bad news, indeed."

"*Now* will you do something about it?" Cyn cried. "Our people must start training for war. Swords must be forged and armor repaired. We can't afford to be caught off guard."

Musicians approached, strumming more of their stringed instruments and singing a merry drinking song. Distracted, the king watched them, his fingers tapping to the rhythm.

"Father," Cyn said, "Deirdre and I have a present for you." He looked at his sister. "Give it to him," he said bitterly. "Don't you know toys are the most important thing in Metgarde?"

When Deirdre pulled out a pair of mechanical metal ducks and set them on the table, the king gave a cry of joy. He immediately wound them up and set them to walking across the table. They quacked and waddled, paused, quacked and waddled again. Their beaks opened and closed, and their eyes rolled.

"Marvelous!" the king cried. "Delightful!"

"If you'll excuse me," Cyn said. He stalked away.

Deirdre glanced at her mother, then rose as well. "Come on, Maria." Turning, she hurried after Cyn.

Maria followed them out a side door. Cyn was leaning against the wall with a glum expression on his face. He made a fist and pounded it against his thigh. "I know what *I'm* doing," Cyn said. "I'm going to scout the land, warn a few villages about the new trog threat."

"I understand," Deirdre said. "You mean Mother's people."

Cyn grinned at her. "Them especially. If the king can't save us, look to the queen, right?"

"What are you talking about?" Maria said.

"Well . . ." Deirdre paused. "Our mother, the queen, isn't from this city. She's the daughter of the Duke of Marshland. The marsh elves have always been a bit wild, kind of roguish. The duke might help rally our people. Lost causes appeal to him."

"Besides," Cyn said, "I haven't been to Marshland in years. It might be fun to see our cousins and aunts and uncles again."

"Can I come?" Maria asked.

"It's a three-week trip across the marshes, and the trail tends to be a bit, well, *wet*," he said. "But if you want to learn to ride, this is the perfect chance. I'll be there to help."

Maria said, "What about Charlie and the others?"

"They'll come, too, of course."

"And you?" Maria asked Deirdre.

"I don't think so," Deirdre said. "I'm going to stay here and talk to the queen. If anyone can get her moving against the trogs, I can."

Cyn stood up straighter. "Then we leave tomorrow morning at dawn."

8

At sunrise, a party of six assembled in front of the stables. The morning breeze carried a cool edge, and Maria wrapped a wool cloak over the riding habit she had borrowed from Deirdre. Cyn and the others dressed as they always did, but with short swords at their sides and knives in their belts.

"I'll get the horses," Charlie said, and he vanished into the stables. Cyn began checking over the provisions and baggage.

Maria and Deirdre both yawned. The previous night they had stayed up late packing clothes, provisions, and herbal medicines, including muscle ointments and a sour-smelling herbal insect repellent that Deirdre insisted Maria would need for the trip.

"And what do I need these for?" Maria asked. She touched the gold earrings and spiral bracelets that Deirdre had given her. "Are they magic?"

"No," Deirdre said, "you just look pretty in them." Maria blushed.

Charlie appeared leading five horses and four mules with long ears and blunt heads. While Charlie, Felix, and Shane tied their baggage on the mules' backs, Deirdre led a large gray horse over to Maria. "Meet

Bluebell," she said, rubbing the horse's nose. "She's as gentle as they come."

"She's so big," Maria said. The animal's back looked dauntingly high off the ground.

Deirdre made a step for her by linking her fingers together. "Let me give you a hand up. Just put your left foot here, and I'll lift you up." When Maria looked at her doubtfully, Deirdre added, "Trust me. She's so gentle you'd have to throw yourself to the ground to fall off her back."

Maria swallowed the doubts rising inside her. Taking a deep breath, she stepped onto Deirdre's hand and let the girl help swing her up into the saddle.

"See?" Deirdre said, looking up at Maria. "It's not so hard. You'll be fine, even without me along to help you."

Deirdre bent down to adjust the length of the stirrups and pushed Maria's toes into them. "Just keep your feet there. Don't worry, Bluebell's a real follower. She'll tag along without you doing much work."

Cyn stood by his own black stallion that pranced impatiently. He swung into the saddle in a single fluid motion. He's been doing it for years, Maria reminded herself.

"Let's go!" Cyn called. "Good-bye, Deirdre."

"Say hello to all my cousins for me!" Deirdre said.

"I will," Maria promised. "Bye!"

Bluebell trotted after Cyn and the others, and Cyn coached Maria as they rode. "Slide your feet further into the stirrups," he said. "Now sit forward a bit more . . . that's right!"

Sure enough, sitting on the horse suddenly felt better to Maria. Now, instead of jolting up and down with Bluebell's every step, she rode with the horse's gait.

Charlie circled around and flanked her on the left, while Felix and Shane ranged ahead, whooping and racing up the road. "You're doing great," Charlie said. "Nothing to worry about."

She gave him a faint smile. "I think I'm starting to get seasick!" He laughed and rode ahead to join his friends.

As the morning grew brighter and warmer, the riders passed through the outskirts of the settled lands. Maria looked back at Cyn. "Can you explain how time works differently in this world? Charlie says he was born over a hundred and thirty years before I was . . . and he thinks he's only been here a year."

Cyn shrugged. "What year it is in your world depends on *where* we go into it. Earth and Faery overlap in many places at different times. It's magic. How else can I explain it?"

"So I really can go back to my own world, and my mom won't have missed me?"

"Right," Cyn said with a reassuring smile. "I've gone back to Charlie's time twice already this year. You should see all the marvelous cannons and muskets they use on their battlefields."

"Then how come he doesn't know about the others or what times they come from? I think Shane is from the 1930s."

"Chicago, in your year 1936, actually. He wanted to be a gangster."

"And what about Felix?"

"San Francisco, in your year 1970."

Maria shook her head in amazement. "I guess I'll take your word for it."

For the first few hours, the ride seemed easy. Bluebell moved at a quiet, comfortable pace, and it was simply a matter of letting the horse do all the work.

The countryside looked calm and unchanged: hilly, with ample fields and orchards, an occasional farmhouse or village. The long dirt road wound ahead.

They stayed at a different inn that night, but Cyn didn't bother trying to warn people about the trogs. "The trogs shouldn't be this far out," he said. "If I needlessly alarm the people now, it might be harder to rouse them when it counts."

Maria did not share his confidence, but that night she contented herself with listening to elves tell stories of the glorious old days of the trog wars, when elves and men banded together and completely destroyed their enemy . . . or so they thought.

Maria awoke with aching muscles the next morning, but the ointment Deirdre had packed eased the worst of her pains, and by lunchtime she was as limber as ever. The rest of the day passed uneventfully. Felix's horse threw a shoe, and he had to double up with Charlie, but they found a blacksmith within the hour and soon the horse was reshod.

The third day brought them to a broad wasteland of marshes. It was a dismal place: Tall yellow-brown grass grew everywhere, spotted with clumps of scraggly trees. Unpleasant smells of decaying vegetation and brackish water hung around them, and wisps of marsh-mist drifted across the pools.

The road grew less well traveled, little more than a pair of ruts with grass growing between them. Where it entered the marsh, the road became a single twisting trail. The boys reined in to form a circle in a clearing. Nobody looked happy about crossing the marsh. Now she could see why Deirdre hadn't wanted to come.

"Is it really going to take us weeks to cross that?" Maria asked.

Cyn nodded. "It's slow going and the trail twists and turns. We probably won't make more than a few miles' progress a day. Ah, well. *C'est la vie!*"

"That's French!" she protested.

Felix chuckled. "I taught him that one. Pretty cool, huh?"

"It fits the situation better than any elvish expression," Cyn said. "We'd better set the riding order. I'll go first, then Maria, then Charlie. Shane, you go fourth, and Felix can be our rear guard."

"Roger," Felix said.

"Why *do* you keep saying that?" Charlie demanded. "There's nobody here by that name."

Felix frowned at him. "That's what you're *supposed* to say when the chief gives you a command."

Muttering something that sounded like "Yankee smart aleck," Charlie turned his horse and headed for the mouth of the marsh trail. Felix flashed Maria the thumbs-up signal.

"Cyn said you were from San Francisco," she said.

"Coolest place on Earth," he replied with a smile. "Groovy."

"Were you a hippie or something?"

"I wish!" He laughed. "It's a really happening scene, but my parents are total squares. I have some love beads and stuff, but mostly I just watched. Sometimes I used to go to Haight-Ashbury with my friends for the parties, and that's neat."

"I wish I'd been there," she said. "It would have been fun."

"Ol' Charlie doesn't believe in fun. He's too worried about the Civil War and he won't listen when I tell him the South lost a hundred years ago," Felix said. "Hey, if you want to really freak him out, just mention television. He insists I made it up."

Inside the marsh, Maria felt her hair droop from the humidity. The swampland sapped their conversation, the riders continued in silence. Maria didn't want to do anything herself but plod along, staring at the ground. Their passage stirred up clouds of insects, but Deirdre's herbal repellent kept them away. The smell of brackish water grew worse, and a thin mist drifted across the trail.

As the sun settled in the west, they climbed a hillock and found themselves in a clearing. Through the thin mist snaking across the ground, Maria could see a circle of stones marking an old firepit. The bare ground looked dry enough for blankets.

Before anyone could dismount, Cyn gave a cry of alarm. "Ambush!" Charlie shouted—too late.

Maria looked around wildly, hearing heavy slurping sounds as massive things emerged from the thick mud. Glistening gray trogs armed with spiked clubs and spears climbed like nightcrawlers out of the muck beside the path. Others waded out from the water surrounding the campsite, sloshing through the mud.

The horses spooked. The black stallion bucked, and Cyn went flying. Charlie and Felix fought to control their mounts while they drew their short swords. Shane's horse bolted into the deep marsh, carrying him off the trail into black water.

Bluebell whirled and stamped, her big eyes rolling and her nostrils flaring. Maria clutched the reins, but couldn't get the horse to stop. With a squealing whinny, the mare plunged off the trail between two large trogs. The trogs both swung at Maria with their clubs, but she ducked low and they missed.

On a nearby hillock in the twilight, she suddenly

saw a slim dark elf with a hideous black mask over his face. He watched the unfolding battle with interest, laughing over the din of combat.

Bluebell shied from the masked elf, plunging deeper into the marsh. Cold water surged over Maria's feet. Too scared to cry out, she clung to the reins. Bluebell found firmer ground and heaved herself through the grass and thorny bushes.

Maria squeezed her eyes closed, and it took a strong effort to pry them open again. "Easy!" she kept pleading. "Whoa, girl!" The sounds of battle rose from far behind her in the trees, but still the mare fled into the uncharted swamp.

The hilly ground ended, and Bluebell plunged into three feet of cold water. The mare half swam, half floundered her way to another little island. Her hooves scrambled on moss and wet sand. She had almost made it to the top when the soft, wet earth caved in under the horse's weight. Bluebell fell with a despairing squeal.

Maria's feet flew from the stirrups, and she landed flat on her back. Muddy water closed over her head. She rose, gasping and sputtering, only a few feet from her horse. Bluebell once more tried to scramble up the steep bank.

Maria grabbed for the horse's trailing reins. She missed and slid deeper into the muck. When she tried to climb to her feet, seesawing her arms wildly for balance, she fell back with a splash.

Bluebell had solid ground under her hooves again. She took off at a gallop through the thick weeds and overhanging branches. In seconds the mare had vanished into the darkness.

Maria shivered. She was cold, soaking wet, and sitting in six inches of mud and water. She didn't know whether to cry, scream, or laugh hysterically.

She sat catching her breath for a few moments before she finally managed to pull herself to dry land. She'd twisted her left ankle, and she felt a twinge of pain in her right shoulder when she moved her arm.

She wrung brown water from her hair, wiped her face on her wet shirttails, and emptied water from her shoes. Then she strained to hear noises over the hum of insects.

No familiar sounds greeted her ears. When she looked around, she realized she'd become completely disoriented. She had no idea in which direction to find Cyn and the others—if they had defeated the trogs—if they were still alive.

9

Maria forced down her panic and sat down to think, but nothing occurred to her. She didn't know where she was, didn't know which way led out. She didn't even know if her companions had survived the trog ambush.

She decided to wait till dawn and then look for a farmhouse, no matter how far she had to slog through the damp marsh. But then she saw a strange light a short distance through the thickets of scrub trees. The glow bobbed up and down like a lantern. Maria allowed hope to flutter inside her. Maybe it was Cyn looking for her!

Rising up on sore legs, she watched the light move slowly to the left, as though following a trail. Perhaps the other boys had camped there . . . but it could also be trogs or the masked elf. She'd have to be careful.

Feeling her way, Maria crept toward the light, sometimes wading into knee-deep cold, dark water, sometimes scrambling across bushy hillocks. Occasionally she lost sight of the flickering glow, but each time it came back into view.

After what seemed like hours, Maria stopped, panting. She'd been following that light an awfully long time, and she should have reached it by now.

Exhausted, she climbed to the top of a hillock and sank down between two gnarled, moss-covered trees. Flies buzzed around her head. With the image of the two murderous trogs lunging at her as Bluebell crashed between them, she finally began to cry. She didn't think she'd ever been so miserable in her life, not even when the mugger had chased her through the fog. She'd been *scared* then. Now she was also upset, wet, cold, hungry, and sore. And lost. She might die. Her friends might already be dead. She might never see her family again. She could be attacked by trogs at any moment—

Something touched her leg. She jerked back with a start, afraid of snakes. Instead of a snake, though, she saw dozens of shimmering dragonflies gathered around her. They glowed pale yellow, luminous as fireflies. Their delicate wings buzzed like sheets of diamond paper. Their large eyes looked like pearls, shining and metallic. The dragonflies swiveled their round heads on supple necks, gazing at her with insect eyes. A few more of the glowing bugs fluttered down from the branches.

The light—she'd been following one of them through the trees! She gave a nervous laugh, and the dragonflies zipped back out of sight, humming and buzzing to each other. With a high vibrating tone, the noise seemed to form . . . words. After a few seconds, the dragonflies peered out at her from behind leaves and tree trunks.

"I won't hurt you," Maria said.

Only one insect—bolder than the rest—stayed as the others dashed off into the trees. The bold dragonfly alighted on Maria's knee, eight inches from her face. He swiveled his head from one side to the other, as if studying her features.

"Hello," Maria whispered.

"Hello," he buzzed back, cocking his head. "Hello, hello, hello!"

"Do you understand me?" she asked.

"Do you understand me?" he said in a perfect imitation of her words. His insect mandibles moved sideways as he spoke.

They continued to stare at each other until Maria sighed and let her head slump forward. "I'm too tired for this."

"You do look a mess," the little voice said.

Maria's head jerked up. The glowing dragonfly jumped up and hovered in the air, staring at her with his big round eyes.

"You *do* understand!" Maria said. "You're a friend!"

"Yes," he agreed. "Friend. That's my name."

"Friend?" she said. "My name is Maria. I've lost my friends—my other friends, I mean—and my horse, and my way. Can you help me get out of the marsh?"

"Yes," he said.

"Thank goodness!"

"Can you help me get out of the marsh?" he asked.

Maria sighed in exasperation. "Look, Friend," she said, "I need to get out of here. I'll—I'll give you this." She pulled off one of the delicate spiral earrings Deirdre had given her. In the dim glow of Friend's body it gave a soft golden sheen.

Friend's wings blurred with pleasure. "Pretty!" he said.

"It's yours if you help me get out of the marsh," she said.

"Okay," he said. Fluttering his wings, he rose in the air, circled once, and returned to sit on Maria's left shoulder.

Maria stood. "Which way?"

"There." Friend pointed straight ahead, away from the hillock and dry ground.

Taking a deep breath, Maria waded into the cold water. She couldn't get any more miserable, she thought, so she might as well take the direct approach.

During the trek, sometimes they were on dry ground, and sometimes they waded so deep that Maria had to swim. Friend flew over her head, calling instructions and encouragement.

Finally, as the eastern sky above the hulking tree-tops grew pale with coming dawn, Maria parted a tall curtain of grass and found herself staring at a little orchard. Cultivated trees had never looked so beautiful before.

"Thank you!" she told Friend.

"Thank you!" he told her back.

Maria removed the spiral earring and held it out to him. He buzzed over, snatched it with his six legs. The added weight made the dragonfly sink toward the ground, but he fluttered his transparent wings furiously until he rose again to hover before her. "Heavy!" he said, then zipped back toward the marsh.

Maria sat down, poured water and mud from each shoe, and wrung out her riding habit. She looked up and down the orchard but had no idea which direction led to the road to Metgarde. Finally she just turned right and began to walk.

Twenty minutes later she spotted the rutted path— after the trackless patches of the swamps, it looked like a highway. She saw with joy that several horses and two mules were tied under a tree nearby. Around a small campfire sat Charlie and Felix.

"Miss Maria!" Charlie called, standing. "We were worried about you. What happened?"

"I'm all right," she said, looking around. "My horse bolted, and I got lost. Where are Cyn and Shane?"

The two boys exchanged grim glances. "The trogs got 'em," Felix finally said.

The next days were a nightmare for Maria. She changed into dry clothes from one of the two pack mules and ate a spartan breakfast. After that, the three of them rode back toward Metgarde.

She felt herself drifting. Everything receded to some distant place: riding, riding, and more riding, hardly stopping to eat or drink or rest. Through it all she kept seeing Cyn being thrown from his horse, and the bloodthirsty trogs wading ashore to grab him, the dark masked elf laughing in the shadows. . . .

She sat in shock, not paying enough attention to the work of riding. Every muscle in her body ached in a way she'd never felt before. She wished she could curl up and die.

By noon on the second day, they finally made it to Metgarde's gates. It seemed a cruel irony, but Cyn's dire warnings had begun to sink in: Two elves now stood on guard duty in the brightly painted tower, but they barely raised their eyes as Charlie, Felix, and Maria rode past.

They headed straight for the keep. For once there didn't seem to be any festival in progress, although banners and garlands were being strung for the next one.

They entered the keep through the main gates. Charlie dismounted in front of the stables as two young elves came running to lead their horses off. Maria needed to be helped from the saddle, and her knees locked whenever she tried to walk. She didn't think even Deirdre's magical ointment would help her now.

"Oh, what in tarnation am I going to tell the king?" Charlie said, sounding as numb inside as Maria felt. "You have to come with me, Miss Maria. Please."

Maria swallowed. "Okay." Her voice sounded tight, and she felt a hollowness in her chest. She straightened, forcing her head and shoulders back. "We'd better do it now, first thing."

"Right," Felix agreed.

Maria led the way up the stone steps and into the huge hall. The unused suits of armor on display seemed an ironic twist.

The king sat on his throne, surrounded by elves with long gray beards. The queen leaned forward on the lower throne next to him, listening raptly. When the queen saw the grimy visitors approach, a look of alarm crossed her face. She touched the king's arm, and he looked up, too.

"Where is my son?" the queen asked.

Maria swallowed. "I . . . your majesty . . . I'm sorry, but . . ." Slowly Maria, Charlie, and Felix stammered out the tragic tale of the trog ambush and the trek back through the marsh to Metgarde. When they finished, both the king and queen sat as still as statues, their faces ashen.

"It's all true about the trogs, then?" the queen said. "You're certain?"

"How many times do we have to say it?" Charlie said, raising his voice. He looked down in embarrassment. "Uh, begging your pardon, ma'am."

The king finally said, "There can be no peace, no compromise, and no mercy." He rose on creaking legs. His voice filled the audience hall like thunder.

"We hereby declare war on the traitorous elf Mask,

the trogs, and all who serve them!" He slumped back on his throne. "Let the word go out for an army to assemble in the fields outside of Metgarde. All able-bodied elves are to gather their weapons, provisions for a month, and whatever else they need for this campaign. We will march on Mask's fortress—and this time there will be no surviving trogs!"

His men let out a cheer, and Charlie and Felix managed weak applause of their own. Maria swallowed. It was hard to believe Cyn and Shane were both gone.

Deirdre stepped forward from a shadowy alcove. "Come with me," she said, giving Maria a long look that seemed to imply she had more to say. "I'll help you get cleaned up."

Maria excused herself and followed Deirdre along a small corridor to an empty sitting room with a fire burning on the hearth. Deirdre locked the door behind them.

"The king received an ultimatum from Mask this morning," Deirdre said. "The trogs have already declared war on Metgarde! They demanded their ancestral lands back. The court advisors were taking the letter as a joke until you told your tale. Now, it's all too real."

"What else did the letter say?" Maria asked.

"That Mask and his trogs are marching on Metgarde unless the king surrenders immediately. Their terms are monstrous—all elves will be made slaves to the trogs."

Maria shuddered, remembering the sluggish, mud-covered brutes that had come shambling after her.

"But at least we know where they are," Deirdre went on. "Mask and his trogs have made their headquarters in an abandoned fortress at Colcorne Gorge.

If the king can raise his army, he can trap them there, take back the fortress, and finally destroy the trogs and Mask once and for all."

"What about Cyn and Shane?" Maria asked. "If the trogs want slaves, do you think they'd keep them alive?"

"The letter made no mention of ransom, and that can't be a good sign. Cyn would be worth a great deal."

"Oh," Maria said unhappily.

Deirdre leaned forward and whispered harshly, "I have to know this, Maria . . . was it dark when the attack came? Was there a fog or a mist of any kind?"

"What are you getting at?" Maria demanded.

Deirdre swallowed. "I . . . I was hoping Cyn might still be free. He might have escaped."

"But Charlie and Felix saw the trogs take him!"

"Maria, he's a mist-mage, remember? Whenever there's the slightest mist or fog, he can control it, shape it, give it form and substance, make illusions. Maybe he could fool them."

"That's right!" Maria said, remembering.

"I shouldn't be saying this, since he swore me to secrecy," Deirdre whispered, "but Cyn is one of the most powerful magic-users in Faery. He can take mist and shape it, *change* it, so it looks like anyone or anything. He can make his illusions appear solid and real. He could have called up a hundred elven fighting men from the mist on a second's notice. Mask could never have caught Cyn, if there was a mist to work with. At least, that's what I hope."

"There *was* a mist," Maria said slowly. "It wasn't thick, not like the fog in Philadelphia, and it was very low to the ground."

Deirdre paced the warm sitting room, frowning.

"Cyn has always been reckless," she said, "and he has bent the truth on more than one occasion. It would be just like him to help everyone else escape, then follow Mask to discover his camp."

"What about Shane?"

"Perhaps he couldn't be saved, or he got lost like you did."

Maria nodded. "I didn't actually see the trogs grab him. He was thrown from his horse, and then the trogs closed in on him. My own horse bolted. I was too busy trying to hold on." She could just see Cyn doing something as foolhardy and heroic as trying to follow Mask and the trogs. The breath caught in her throat. She allowed herself to hope that Cyn might still be alive.

10

Deirdre crossed her arms in determination. "We've got to go find him. If he's on foot, it could take him weeks to get back from the marsh. Maybe he's counting on us to figure it out. What if he's injured and needs help?"

Maria looked away nervously. She didn't look forward to another trip to the wet, miserable, and frightening marsh. "But if you think he's alive, shouldn't we tell the king and queen? Maybe some troops can hunt for Cyn."

"I can't tell them! I promised Cyn not to let on how powerful his magic is. And I can't let my mother begin to hope—if Cyn really is dead, it would devastate her all over again. You saw her face. Besides, the king needs his soldiers here, to help whip the army into shape for the battle against Mask."

Maria said, "But what if we run into trogs ourselves?"

"If we see any sign of them, we'll turn back right away."

"Deirdre . . ." Maria sighed. "You elves have lived so long without any real threat that you don't believe in danger anymore."

"Now you're sounding like Cyn!" Deirdre said. "If

my brother needs me, I'm not going to let him down. Are you coming—or do I have to go alone?"

"All right," Maria said. She squeezed Deirdre's hand in a show of support. "I guess I owe him that much, too. If he really did follow Mask back to the trogs' camp, we need to find out what he learned."

Maria spent an hour soaking in a hot tub, then took a short nap beneath the satiny sheets in her room as Deirdre packed for their secret quest.

Too soon gentle hands shook her. "Maria!" Deirdre's voice whispered. "Maria!" Maria blinked at her blearily. Deirdre held a candle in one hand and a fresh riding habit in the other. "It's midnight. Time to go. I have clothes for you."

Ten minutes later, the two girls crept down a back stairway. They kept their voices hushed and their footfalls light, tiptoeing down the cold stone steps. They paused at corners to make sure the coast was clear. Four times they had to wait for servants to pass before proceeding; twice they had to turn back and find other routes because of noisy battle preparations.

The castle was in an uproar from the declaration of war. Young and old elves emptied dusty armories, sharpened swords, checked and mended suits of armor. Just a few days earlier, the elves would have spent the entire night dancing, telling stories by roaring fires, or toasting each other's health in merry celebration. Now the gentle, sleepy people were energized, as if they'd been waiting for this all along but hadn't known it.

Finally they reached darkened kitchens, which led to a servants' entrance. The wooden door creaked as Deirdre pushed it open, but no one came forward to investigate. Deirdre and Maria slipped out into the dew-spattered courtyard. A water well covered by a flat square of wood planking stood near the door. Maria could see the back of the stables near the wall. The night was very dark, and the air felt cool and crisp.

Stars filled the black sky like a snowstorm, millions of bright points of light in strange constellations. In her own city, Maria had never seen more than a few of the brightest stars, because the haze of pollution and bright street lights washed out the skies.

They inched toward the stables across the courtyard, keeping to the shadows. Still they saw no one outside. "You'd think they would at least post guards," Maria whispered, "with all the panic the trogs are causing."

"They still haven't remembered everything," Deirdre said. "We haven't had a war in centuries, remember."

As they neared the wooden building, Maria heard horses shifting restlessly, blowing and nickering. She could smell fresh hay and the musky smells of horse sweat and manure—but something was wrong. Soft light oozed from the shuttered windows.

She and Deirdre exchanged questioning glances. "Someone's in there!" Maria whispered.

Several sets of hooves clattered on the floor. Hinges squealed as a stall door opened. Someone spoke in a soothing voice, and another soft voice answered. Not deep, slurred trog grumbles: These sounded like human—or elven—voices. Maria strained to hear, but couldn't make out the words.

Deirdre pulled her to the side, ducking away from the stable doors. With her knees bent and shoulders stooped, Maria and Deirdre crept to the window to peer between the shutter's slats.

Inside, with grim expressions, Charlie and Felix saddled two horses by the dim orange glow of a lantern. The horses stirred uneasily, stamping the straw on the floor. Charlie tightened the cinches around their bellies and checked their reins.

"What are *they* doing here?" Deirdre asked.

Maria gently put a finger to Deirdre's lips. "Watch!"

Charlie extinguished the lantern, then held the horses' reins as Felix tugged open one of the broad plank doors. Charlie led both mounts out, then Felix pushed the stable door shut again. Both boys swung up into the saddles.

"Ready?" Charlie said in a low voice. His blond hair looked silver under the starlight. They rode black horses and dressed in dark clothes, as if they wanted to hide in the darkness.

"Pull up your hood," Felix said.

The boy from the Civil War did so, and his pale face seemed to float in the air. When he turned away from Maria, he all but vanished in the darkness.

"No talking till we're outside the city," Charlie said. "This is the last assignment, so let's really get 'em riled up."

"Cool!" Felix said. He sounded jubilant. Without a backward glance, they rode through the open gates of the keep and out into the sleeping city of elves.

The girls waited until the sounds of the horses vanished in the distance before rising. "Do you think they're going out to look for Cyn?" Deirdre asked. Her large eyes glittered in the faint light. "Do you think they figured it out, too?"

Maria frowned. "They mentioned an assignment," she said. "That doesn't sound like a rescue mission to me." She met Deirdre's gaze. "Maybe Cyn gave them special instructions before the trogs got him. They're up to something."

"Let's follow and see where they're going," Deirdre said, heading for the stable door. "I'll saddle our horses."

Because of the need for speed, they didn't waste time being quiet. Maria helped as best she could, putting their possessions into saddlebags and tying their packs in place. At last, the two led their own horses out to the courtyard, mounted, and headed after Charlie and Felix, riding in silence.

The city streets were deserted. They crossed empty squares where the garlands and festive decorations sagged, damp with dew and night mist. They passed through a small side gate onto a dirt road leading into the countryside. Maria rose in her saddle, peering ahead, straining to see in the darkness.

"There they are!" Deirdre whispered. "Right by the forest—see?" She pointed.

Charlie and Felix were dark shadows inching along the road, most visible when they passed dry fields of yellow hay.

"They're heading down the King's Way," Deirdre said. She touched her heels to her horse's side and started forward. "There aren't any other paths for miles. We'll catch up on the other side of the forest."

"That's not the direction of the marshes," Maria said.

"There's a crossroad about twenty miles from here," Deirdre said. "Perhaps that's the way they intend to go."

"Or maybe they're up to something else entirely," Maria said.

They entered a tangled ribbon of forest. The King's Way narrowed, and Maria ducked her head to keep from hitting her head on low branches. Creepy night sounds echoed from either side, and she glanced around warily. She glimpsed wide yellow eyes staring at her. *It's only animals*, she kept telling herself. Shivering, she urged her horse to a faster pace.

Finally the forest fell away into rolling hills. The road grew wide again, with neatly planted orchards on either side. A scattering of low buildings stood to the left: Small fieldstone-and-mortar farmhouses inhabited by poorer elves nestled among storage sheds, a barn, and outbuildings. Maria smelled cattle and chickens but saw no candlelight winking from the windows. The farm lay fast asleep. The world was silent and peaceful except for the drone of insects.

Deirdre suddenly reined in her mare. "There they are," she said. "What are they doing? Can you see?"

Maria followed Deirdre's gaze. Two figures in black moved like ghosts among the rickety storage sheds of hay and grain. A cow lowed frantically, and chickens began to squawk. A flare of candlelight came on in the farmhouse, then a second and a third. The cow lowed again.

"Should we go and investigate?" Deirdre asked.

Maria felt uneasiness like a cold winter drizzle down her back. "Let's just watch for a few minutes," she said, remembering the mugger on the streets of Philadelphia, and the other dangers to which Deirdre and the other elves seemed completely oblivious.

Deirdre leaned forward in her saddle, and Maria was afraid she was going to call out. She urgently squeezed Deirdre's arm to keep her quiet. "Not a good idea," she said in a low voice.

"But what are they doing?" Deirdre asked. "I want to know."

"I smell smoke!" Maria said.

As if in answer, a yellow glow began to rise from the walls of the barn, accompanied by a dry sound like crinkling paper. Sharp tongues of flame licked out of cracks in the rickety walls, biting through the dense thatched roof. Even damp with dew, the old straw ignited quickly.

More flames flickered to life inside one of the sheds, spreading quickly to the walls, then the roof. Suddenly the whole building blazed. A second shed followed suit, then a third.

"We need to sound the alarm," Maria said. She shouted, "Help! Fire, fire!"

But elves were already spilling from the stone farmhouses in various stages of undress, calling instructions. Many held thick blankets to beat at the flames. Others formed a bucket brigade at the well. Still more darted into the barn and loosed the trapped cows and horses, who bolted into the night.

"Trogs!" someone began shouting. "It's the trogs!"

Hooves thundered nearby, and two figures on black horses galloped down the road away from Metgarde, making little attempt at silence.

"Charlie and Felix did that!" Deirdre said with a cold fury in her voice. "They're no more than common outlaws."

"You don't think that was Cyn's assignment, do you?"

Deirdre glared at her. "Of course not."

Maria said nothing, but she began to have doubts in the back of her mind. Nothing made sense. There had to be a plan at work here—a plan she just didn't quite understand."

"We've got to catch them," she said, nudging her horse. The mare started forward at an obliging trot toward other farmhouses up the road.

Deirdre caught up easily, though she often looked back over her shoulder at the flurry around the blazing farmhouses. "I just can't believe the boys *did* that," she said. "Do you think they'll be able to save the farm?"

"Yes," Maria lied. She suspected the straw roof and the flimsy wooden walls of the barn and sheds would be entirely consumed, no matter what the elves did to fight it.

"Oh no," Deirdre breathed as they approached the next small farmstead. Her face looked stricken. "They've done it again!" She kicked her mare to a gallop, and Maria awkwardly tried to follow suit.

Half a mile up ahead, another glow of fire came from old outbuildings. Flames from the burning farm lit the sky with a ruddy orange glow.

Deirdre stopped at the top of the hill. Breathing hard, Maria pulled up alongside. Below, shouting elves careened between buildings, trying to extinguish the fires.

"I don't understand," Maria said. "I can't believe they'd do this with no reason. It *has* to be Cyn's assignment."

"Charlie and Felix were our friends!" Deirdre said, sounding betrayed. "They spent all their time training with Cyn. He trusted them! He would never let them do a thing like this!"

"Well, they just did it," Maria snapped.

"But *why?*" Deirdre wailed.

Maria sat bolt upright as a thought occurred to her. "Maybe they're trying to upset the local farmers. You know the trogs are going to be blamed for this attack."

"But what good will that do?" Deirdre asked. "It doesn't make sense."

"Yes, it does. The king will double his war preparations now. His people are under attack from all sides. One of his sons is apparently dead. You *know* it will just keep him moving. Now he'll never slow down or forget about the trog threat."

"But why should Charlie and Felix care about that?" Deirdre's voice sounded distraught. "They're not elves."

"Come on," Maria said without answering.

They continued to ride, rushing past the second burning farm. Deirdre glanced back with a forlorn expression. Maria just gritted her teeth and kept going.

Ahead, she saw the expanding glow of a third fire. As they approached, she could hear the flames crackling . . . and the familiar sound of dark horses galloping off into the night.

11

The forest closed in on them again, and it became clear that Charlie and Felix had no intention of stopping for the night.

With branches whipping at their faces and the road taking strange turns, Maria and Deirdre had to slow the horses to a walk.

By now Maria could do a passable job of riding along wide, level roads, but she was not at all good enough to gallop through the forested darkness at a breakneck pace, chasing two shadowy people dressed in black!

The hours wore on as the stars wheeled overhead through the crisscrossed tree branches. Finally, aching and weary, Maria felt ready to drop off her horse. "We've lost them, admit it," she called to Deirdre. "I can't go on. I have to rest. I've been riding for days, remember."

Deirdre sighed. "No sense chasing them any more tonight. Let's rest; then we'll start again at dawn."

Maria eased herself to the ground, groaning with the pins and needles in her legs. They walked their horses until they found a clearing beside the road where they could spread out their blankets and catch a few hours of uncomfortable, restless sleep.

*   *   *

By the time dawn broke through the forest canopy, Maria's muscles had tightened up. She sat up, stiff and sore, clammy in her damp clothes. She rummaged in her saddlebags until she found the salve Deirdre had packed, then spent ten minutes rubbing it into her arms and legs and back. The two girls found a cold stream nearby and splashed the sleep out of their eyes. After a hasty breakfast of dry biscuits and water, they saddled their horses and set out again with new determination.

Deirdre found fresh hoofprints in muddy patches on the road but soon lost the tracks in a confusion of wheel ruts and trampled weeds along the pathway. She dismounted at a small crossroads just before noon and pointed out another set of fresh prints.

"I think it's them," she said, remounting. "They're heading toward the marshes."

Maria nodded, tugging dark, sweat-dampened hair out of her eyes. "I thought so. This must have something to do with Cyn."

They spent another night on the trail, sleeping under the dense protection of a weeping willow that enclosed them like a tent with its drooping branches. All night the whiplike fronds rattled together like old bones, and the wind whispered with a soft laughing sound that kept Maria awake.

She shivered and wished for her warm bed back in the elf king's castle in Metgarde—or even for her cramped little room back in Philadelphia with her baby brother crying all night, and her mother and stepfather staying up late just to have more time to argue. Anything would have been better than this.

The terrain changed rapidly the next day. The

horses picked their way along a path that dwindled to an overgrown, muddy track between trees with brownish algae-covered puddles on either side. Several times glistening orange-and-black snakes crawled across their path. Lizards, trying to catch scant sun on flat rocks, scuttled back into the undergrowth. Fat yellow spiders hung in the middle of fanlike webs that glistened with mist drops; they looked sluggish and well fed from the clouds of mosquitoes and gnats that buzzed around Maria's head.

Finally, late that afternoon, they reached a familiar-looking hillock. "This is where the trogs ambushed us!" Maria cried.

"Let's tie the horses here," Deirdre said. "We need to have a look around. Maybe we'll find a clue."

Maria frowned skeptically. "I don't know anything about tracking. I was trying out for the school play, not girl scouts."

Deirdre's cinnamon-colored hair hung limp and tangled around her delicate elfin face. "Just do the best you can. You might see something that I miss."

Careful not to lose themselves, Maria and Deirdre spiraled outward from the site of the ambush. She found the place they'd stopped their horses, as well as the tracks Bluebell had made as she plunged into the marsh. But there were no real signs of the trog attack, no broken spears or lost clubs, no snapped branches or even much trampled grass.

Maria shook her head in confusion. "*Dozens* of them attacked us, digging out of the muck. Shouldn't they have left a trail as big as a highway?"

"They're not as clumsy as they seem," Deirdre said.

They moved slowly, keeping their eyes to the ground. Maria listened for sounds that didn't belong in the marshes, acutely aware that the hideous trogs might come back at any time.

She saw a humpy, grass-covered island off to the side—she thought it was where she'd seen the masked dark elf laughing during the attack. As she tried to step across, though, her foot slipped and plunged into the icy water up to the ankle. Maria yanked it out, looking in disgust at the green slime now stuck to the leather boot.

"Maria!" Deirdre called from ahead. "I've found something!"

Her boot squishing, Maria trotted around a clump of knobby trees to a solid-looking rise. "Look," Deirdre said, pointing to a bit of bright red cloth caught on a bramble. She pulled it free and handed it to Maria, raising her eyebrows. "Recognize this?"

Maria turned it over in her hand. It glittered with a tiny checker-work of silver threads. "From Cyn's cape?" she asked. "But we're about a quarter mile from the ambush site."

Deirdre nodded. "That means he moved. He got this far!"

Working outward, they saw flattened grass and solid earth stretching away toward the edge of the swamps. Even before Deirdre pointed them out, Maria noticed the hoofprints. They had trampled a clear path through the tall marsh grasses.

"Two horses," Deirdre said.

"Felix and Charlie?" Maria said.

"It has to be," Deirdre said. "The tracks are too recent to be from Cyn and Shane." She looked around, then went to the tallest tree at the top of the hillock. "Let's take a look. Maybe we can see where they're headed." The branches were low and twisted, like a ladder, and she climbed ten feet with little trouble. "Come on up," Deirdre said.

Maria climbed awkwardly, but soon she stood on the branch next to Deirdre, bracing herself against the twisted trunk. She hadn't had much chance to climb trees in Philadelphia.

In the distance, the trail split, with one track continuing deeper into the dense marshes, while the other led toward grassy plains and distant craggy mountains. Charlie and Felix had gone toward the mountains.

"What's over there?" Maria said. "Why would they want to go that direction?"

Deirdre swallowed and didn't say anything for a long moment. Finally she whispered, "Colcorne Gorge—where the trogs are supposed to be, where Mask has set up his fortress for his war against the elves. Maybe Charlie and Felix plan to rescue Cyn."

"Or join him for some secret mission," Maria said. She began to climb down, alternately helping Deirdre and being helped.

After they reached the ground, Deirdre suddenly called out. Maria whirled, expecting trogs, but instead saw dozens of brilliant, glowing dragonflies fluttering around Deirdre. In the daylight their long insect bodies were pale as milk, and their wings moved in a blurry flutter.

Maria laughed with delight. "Friend!"

"Friend!" one of them called back. He broke away from the others and flew to Maria's side, then perched on her shoulder. "Hello, hello, hello!" he said. The other glowing dragonflies whirred and buzzed around the two girls.

"Have you seen any trogs?" Maria asked Friend.

"Bring present!" he said.

"I have a present for you," she said. "But first you have to tell me about the trogs."

"What trogs?"

"Big, ugly creatures with clubs. They crawl out from underground. They were here a week ago. Have you seen them?"

"No trogs here!" Friend chirped happily. "Give present now?"

"Here," Maria said, offering him the bit of red cloth from Cyn's cape. Friend took it and cooed, then fluttered away from her. The other insects followed.

"How did you do that?" Deirdre asked wonderingly. "How can you talk to them?"

Maria looked at her in bewilderment. "I just spoke and they answered. Couldn't you hear him?"

"No," Deirdre admitted. "All I heard were little chirping noises." Then she grinned happily. "Maria, I think we've found your magic talent—you're a talker! You can talk to the dragonflies!" She shook her head in admiration. "That's a one-in-a-thousand talent. You're very lucky."

Maria felt happiness welling inside her. "I didn't know I was doing anything special."

"Then you must be very talented indeed. I've always had to work at my spinning," Deirdre said. "You know, if there aren't any trogs around, we should be able to follow Charlie and Felix at a fast pace—perhaps even catch up with them."

"Good. Then we can find out what they know about Cyn," Maria said.

Three days of slow travel brought them out of the marsh. Each night Friend and the shining dragonflies came to Maria, bringing her berries, bits of straw, and bright pebbles as presents. Maria gave away all of their jewelry before realizing it wasn't *what* she gave that mattered to the dragonflies, but just the act of giving. After that, she gave them back the pebbles they'd already given her, and everyone was happy.

They camped just outside the marshes, on sweeping grasslands that extended to a line of mountains at the horizon. It was wonderful to be on dry ground at last, Maria thought as she rolled herself in a blanket for the night, her breath misting in the air. Then she saw a solitary glow over her head and looked up to see Friend peering down at her from the branches of the tree.

"What are you doing here?" she asked.

"What are you doing here?" Friend asked back.

"I'm going with Deirdre."

"I'm going with Deirdre, too."

"You'd better stay in the swamp, where it's safe," Maria said.

"Yes?"

"Yes."

Friend vanished in a sudden flutter of wings. Maria sighed and closed her eyes. She was asleep in seconds.

They rode for two days across miles of level grasslands, nearing the jutting crags that looked like broken teeth. A sliver of moon hung low in the sky, shedding pale light as the sunset faded into glorious colors.

"We'd better not camp," Deirdre suggested. "We should ride across the rest of these wide-open plains under cover of darkness so that the trogs don't see us. We can reach the cover of the mountains and get to Colcorne Gorge by about midnight."

"What about trogs?" Maria said. "If we get too close, we might be captured!"

"Don't be afraid," Deirdre said. She patted her mare on the neck. "We have horses. If they so much as scent trogs, they'll run for their lives—you've seen how sluggish the trogs are."

"I guess." Maria had no great desire to ride all night long again. She felt sore and hungry, and she wanted nothing more than to soak in a hot bath. But she was intrigued now, and curiosity won out over her natural caution. She urged her horse forward. "Let's go, then."

As the sky darkened, their horses' legs made hissing sounds as they trotted through mile after mile of tall dry grass. Maria dozed in the saddle, nuzzling her cheek against the horse's soft mane. They made excellent time across the flatlands, pausing only once at a winding clear stream that cut through the plain for the horses to refresh themselves.

As they climbed a rocky hill, Maria looked back toward the edges of the plains and saw, far in the distance, the flickering lights of campfires. "Is that the king's army?" she asked. "Is he already marching on Colcorne Gorge?"

Deirdre shook her head. "It can't be the whole army, not yet. It must be an advance scouting party to test the trogs' strengths and defenses. They may complicate matters for us, or they may provide a diversion." She straightened and faced forward with determination.

The stars continued their slow pinwheel overhead. Maria watched the sharp line of mountains rise higher in front of her. The black barrier cut off the horizon, leaving only a jagged silhouette against the sky. Somewhere in those forbidding cliffs stood the fortress of a traitorous elf and his army of trogs—and Cyn himself had gone there to stop them. . . .

In the middle of the night, the horses passed into a craggy canyon, winding toward the towering keep of the trogs. Rounding a corner, they saw firelight twinkling like angry red eyes far up a cliffside.

"That must be it!" Maria said in a low voice.

Deirdre nodded. "We'd better leave the horses here. We don't want the trogs hearing us."

"But you said we would ride away if—"

Deirdre looked at her. "I've come to save my brother, Maria, and I'm not leaving without him. If you're afraid, I'll do it myself. Just ride back to the king's army. They'll take care of you."

Maria stared into her friend's determined eyes. True, the girls did have surprise on their side. And it was dark . . . perhaps they could go a little farther into the gorge without being seen. "All right," she said.

Deirdre said, "I won't forget what you're doing, Maria."

They left their horses hobbled in a small side canyon, then proceeded on foot. As they drew nearer to where the fires burned, Maria began to make out the sharp outlines of the trog fortress. Jutting out from the solid rock of the cliff face, the structure seemed to be all sharp angles, pointed spires, and jutting towers like demons' horns curving away from the rock. Behind, tunneled deep into the rock of the mountainside, were labyrinths of passages to larger trog colonies far underground.

"We'd better not talk unless we can't help it," Deirdre whispered. "They must have guards posted."

Maria agreed. They crept forward, pressing themselves against the vertical rock walls, gliding from shadow to shadow. Maria could discern paths cut into the cliff face, steep switchbacks wide enough for

"Come with me. I have a lot to tell you, and a lot more to show you." He helped the girls up the first step onto the steep trog road.

"Charlie, Felix, and I still have a great many preparations to make before dawn," Cyn continued. "This is our last night before the king's vanguard gets to the gorge. Come on, it's a long hike. There are 1,108 steps—I've counted every single one of them. And the hard part is, they're too tall because they were built for the trogs. You'll find your legs aching by about step 200 or so, but it's the only way up to the battlements."

"Cyn, I want to know what you've been doing," Deirdre said. "We thought you were dead—"

He waved his finger at her. "Save your breath, dear sister. You'll need your energy for the long climb. We'll talk over something to drink when we get to the battlements."

Under the waning moonlight, they began their arduous climb. Maria's legs ached after the fiftieth step, but she bit her lip and pushed onward. The blackness of Colcorne Gorge seemed absolute, with silence broken only by a rustling wind scraping along the stark cliffs. No insects chirruped; no birds made night noises; no moths or bats swooped overhead.

Maria's legs began to cramp, and she paused to massage her calf muscles before limping after Cyn and Deirdre. She plodded upward, repeating to herself, Just one more, just one more. Their footsteps echoed on the rocks, and loose stones dislodged from their climb made tap-tapping noises as they fell.

Finally, exhausted, Maria pulled herself up the last step to a small flat area on the gorge wall. A huge gate stood directly before them with a half-raised spiked portcullis.

Time had not been kind to the ancient trog keep. Stone blocks had tumbled out of position as the mortar eroded away. A few tunnels disappearing back into the cliff face had caved in. The place looked more like some long-abandoned ruin than the headquarters of a monstrous army.

"I apologize for the condition of my keep," Cyn said. "The trogs built it about three thousand years ago, and, uh, they weren't exactly master craftsmen. The four of us have restored some of the rooms below, so you should be fairly comfortable."

"Four?" Maria asked.

"Charlie, Felix, Shane, and I," Cyn said, looking surprised. "I thought you knew. Why else did you come here?"

"We *don't* know," Deirdre said, a little harshly. "You haven't explained anything yet!"

"Oh," Cyn said, looking troubled. "Come with me, then." Turning, he led them through the gate. They climbed a smaller set of stairs and emerged onto the top of one of the great lookout towers. A huge bonfire blazed in a stone firepit, snapping and hissing. Sour-smelling smoke hung low to the weathered floor, stirred by occasional breezes. The blaze threw flickering shadows across several massive trog sentries standing at the parapets.

"Have a look at my army!" Cyn said with an expansive gesture.

The trog sentries showed no reaction to Maria and Deirdre. Maria wasn't sure she wanted to see the monsters this close up. How had Cyn gotten them to cooperate with his schemes?

"The most important thing," Cyn continued in a serious voice, "is to keep up appearances. From a distance, the trog fortress looks just as imposing as it

ever did—you saw it on your way up." He moved toward the parapets. "Take a closer look."

"Be careful!" Deirdre said.

Laughing, Cyn stopped before one of the motionless trog sentries. Maria expected to see the great lumpy form reach over and grab him, but the trog didn't react at all.

Cyn gazed appraisingly at the trog, then reached out to grab its waist. "You're tilting a little bit to the left, my friend."

To Maria's astonishment, Cyn straightened the hideous shape like a giant doll, then shifted the trog's arms to hold its battleaxe in a different position. Cyn turned back to them, grinning. "It isn't real. I don't know why you're so nervous."

Deirdre and Maria looked at each other, amazed and exasperated. Approaching, Maria saw that the misshapen forms were just ragged mannequins made out of straw-stuffed sacks and paint and ugly embellishments. They weren't even well made. The paint was garish, the forms too bulky, and even the coarse stitches holding them together showed plainly. But the shadows and her own belief had convinced her that these were real monsters.

When Cyn laughed at their reaction, Deirdre slapped him hard across the face. The sound was like a gunshot in the night silence.

"That's for being cruel, Cyn," she said. Her face boiled with anger. "You had me believing you were dead. The king and queen think the trogs murdered you. How could you do that to us?"

Cyn blinked in surprise. "If the king didn't believe, he would never lift a finger. He always wanted his children to have honorable deaths in battle, just like our ancestors. It's about time he got a war of his very own."

Maria glared at Cyn. "Why are you doing all this?" she said. "It doesn't make sense. The elves have had peace for so long. Why are you wrecking it?"

"What *is* your game here?" Deirdre demanded.

Cyn took his sister's hand. "Let's go down to the warmer rooms where we can discuss this over a nice meal." He raised his eyebrows at Maria. "We elves are terribly civilized, you know."

Deirdre snatched her hand away. "I'm less civilized than you think!"

Cyn poked out his lower lip in a pout. "Maria, you're from Earth. At least *you* should be able to figure it out, even if Deirdre can't. Shane, Felix, and Charlie certainly did. Am I being that devious?"

"Maybe some of us just don't have devious minds," Maria said.

He chuckled, then crossed to the center of the tower and opened a trapdoor, revealing a winding staircase lit by torches.

"Ladies first," Cyn said.

Maria sighed, then went down, and Deirdre followed. Cyn brought up the rear, closing the trapdoor with a hollow *thump* over their heads. Maria felt like a mountain climber as she descended. She never wanted to see another set of stairs in her life.

Clearly, the keep had been deserted for centuries. Inside, the dank odors of mold and decay filled the air. Cobwebs hung from the walls, and dust puffed out under their feet.

Two levels down, the corridor opened into a warm suite of rooms. Cyn and his friends had not only swept it clean, but brought in rugs for the floors and a few old tapestries for the walls. A roaring fire filled the hearth, taking away the stone's chill. Two scrawny chickens sizzled over the flames on a spit, drenching the air with pleasant smells. At a high trog table made of rough petrified wood, Shane sat in a broad high-backed chair, sewing lumpy pillows onto a black trog costume like the ones Felix and Charlie had been wearing.

"Hello, Deirdre, Maria," Shane said, standing.

"That explains what happened to him," Maria said to Deirdre.

"Were you two worried about me?" Shane grinned. "Thank you!"

"It won't happen again," Maria said.

Cyn said, "Why don't you two sit down and I'll get you something to eat?"

"You promised an explanation," Deirdre said, folding her arms stubbornly. "We've waited long enough. Your friends burned several farms a few nights ago. Did you know about that?"

Cyn waved the question aside. "Of course I knew. I gave the orders to do it."

"Why?" Maria demanded.

"To stir up the elves, of course. To get them angry enough for battle—like hitting a hornet's nest with a stick. They needed provocation."

He sat at the trog table and poured himself a cup of thick red wine, which he gulped down before he continued. He motioned for Deirdre and Maria to sit, but they remained standing.

Cyn shrugged. "I was goading the elves, forcing them to take action so they would snap out of that waking sleep they call life. I had to get them so infuriated at the trogs that they'd get up and *fight* instead of sitting around telling stories about a war that ended three hundred years ago."

Maria finally took a seat on the uncomfortable, too-large chair. "Weren't the real trogs causing enough destruction all by themselves? Did you have to add to it?"

Cyn's eyes caught the fire, and he slammed both palms down on the petrified tabletop, making a loud echo in the room. Shane dropped his work in surprise.

"There are no real trogs!" Cyn shouted. "They really *were* all wiped out in the war! Everything you blamed on the trogs, we did ourselves—from burning a few storage barns and scaring some horses to knocking down trees and leaving fake tracks in the dirt!"

Deirdre stared at him in horror. "Abraugh!" she said. "All the dead horses, the slain elves—you killed them? If there are no trogs, that had to be you!"

Cyn scowled at her. "Oh, of course not! There were never any dead elves. The village you thought you saw destroyed is just fine—completely intact. The carnage was simply an illusion I made with the mist that morning. You know I can work magic with the mist. I can make anything seem real if I try."

He steepled his fingers and looked at the two girls across the rough table. "I created that entire burned-out village in a clearing in the forest. Just a shadow play. Then, when we reached the real Abraugh Village, I masked it out, made it look like part of the forest. We rode right through it without your ever knowing we were there. You were so terrified at the time, we didn't even slow down."

Cyn poured himself more wine. "None of this has been real. I gave the elves a fictitious enemy and a target to fight against. Now my father can go out and reclaim some of his lost glory from the Trog Wars."

"That's ridiculous," Deirdre said. "A waste of time and energy. And lives."

"But necessary. The elves, as a race, are dying. We've lost the spark of life, our will to survive and succeed. We haven't done anything worth telling stories about in centuries. Our peace has put us all to sleep! We haven't found other goals or challenges. When the last trog died, when the last elf hero laid down his sword, we entered the twilight of our race. We've begun to fade away, Deirdre. You know it's true."

Deirdre couldn't look him in the eye. "Yes, I know it's true. But that doesn't mean you're doing the right thing. Staging a make-believe war. . . ."

Cyn looked at Maria. "The magical doors to your world used to be wide open—but after the wars, when the elves lost interest, the doors began to close. Humans have always found something to strive for, new battles to fight, new gadgets to invent, new frontiers to settle. But here in Faery we have already done everything we intend to, slayed all the dragons, killed all the trogs, made peace with everyone and everything. Now there's nothing to challenge us—unless I succeed here. This is the last chance for our race!"

"But what do you hope to accomplish?" Deirdre asked.

Cyn grinned and sniffed the air. "Food's done," he said. "We'll talk more later."

"Right." Shane rose to pull the chickens from the fire.

"Go on, Cyn. You can't stop there," Maria said. "What are you planning?"

Shane pulled a hunting knife from his belt and hacked the two chickens in halves. He spread the steaming meat on plates, handing one each to Cyn, Deirdre, and Maria, and taking the last for himself.

Maria didn't feel hungry, but she started to eat with her fingers just to avoid having to watch Cyn.

"Tonight is the last night," Cyn said, chewing on a piece of chicken and licking his fingers. "Everything has come to a climax. My father has brought an advance party to lay siege to this keep. They're at the edge of the plains right now."

"So you sent Felix and Charlie to spy on them," Deirdre said.

"No need to spy on them. I know exactly what the king is doing. He's oh-so-predictable. Felix and Charlie are going to spook a scout or two . . . jump them, then run away. They won't be caught, but a trog sighting will do wonders to keep the army awake. The elves will have to march on my keep tonight, to prevent the trogs from swarming out and attacking first. In the morning, when they enter the gorge, I'll have the morning mists to work illusions with. With my magic I can make it appear that the fortress walls are crawling with trogs." His eyes shone.

"But what will happen when the elves really do attack?" Maria asked. "If your trogs are just illusions, what happens when the army sees there's nothing real to fight? What then?"

Cyn's face wore a secretive smile. "I have a plan for that, too. Don't worry. Come now, hurry up and eat. For your own protection, we'll need to put you in one of the locked rooms. I hope I've convinced you—but I've worked too hard for this to risk interference. Shane and I must finish our preparations."

Deirdre pushed her plate away, and Maria did the same, although a bit reluctantly. She'd been hungrier than she'd thought.

"This way," Cyn said, rising and indicating a door on the far end of the common room. Deirdre and

Maria entered a spacious cell with four long straw beds. Maria guessed this was where Cyn and his friends slept. But the two boys remained outside the door.

Cyn said, "I'm afraid we won't be able to check on you till morning. You might as well go to sleep. We have to work up on the battlements so my father's scouts can see moving forms."

He picked up his hideous black mask, holding onto the sharp spikes around its edge as he placed it on his head. As he did so, Cyn seemed to become an entirely different person.

"Most important of all," he said, "they need to see a certain dark elf called Mask."

Shane pushed the heavy door closed, and in the sudden silence they heard a lock click.

13

Bending, Maria peered through the rusty keyhole. "Hey!" she shouted. "Let us out of here!"

She could see Shane moving around in the firelit common room. He tossed the key onto the petrified table with a *clink*, then followed Cyn out of view down the stone-walled corridors. The key might have been on the other side of the world, for all the good it did them.

Deirdre slumped down on one of the long, creaking beds. She stared miserably at Maria. Tired shadows ringed her eyes. "We've got to stop Cyn. We have to find a way to escape from here."

"Maybe the window?" Maria crept over to the narrow opening, which was just wide enough for trog archers to shoot arrows through. Maria tried to stick her head out, but a fringe of wicked iron spikes protruded outside the frame—either to keep invaders from climbing in, or to keep trogs from escaping.

When Maria looked down, she saw a sheer, dizzying drop. The outer walls of the keep looked smooth as glass, as if sculpted from polished rock, providing no hand- or foothold down to the bottom of Colcorne Gorge. The plunge looked farther even than the 1,108 steps they had climbed to reach the top.

"We're too high up," she said in defeat.

Deirdre sighed. "Then Cyn's won. He's thought of everything. There's nothing to do but wait and hope that nobody gets killed in his crazy game."

Deirdre fell silent for a moment, then continued, "I don't think he understands that his plan will cause more harm than good. He's only thinking of one side of it." She shook her head. "When our father learns there aren't any trogs, when he learns that it's all been a trick, he'll be outraged. He'll feel like a fool. He and all the other elves will heave a great sigh of relief that there really was no threat after all—just as the old storytellers claimed from the start. The trogs are truly dead, and the elves can go back to their slow death. Cyn is right about that part, at least."

Maria saw her point. "It'll be like crying wolf one time too many. And nothing will be able to rouse them next time . . . if there *is* a next time." She leaned against the window and sank her chin in her palms. "Do you know what this other plan of Cyn's could be? He's got something up his sleeve."

Deirdre leaned forward and propped her elbows on her knees. Her forehead furrowed. "I'm trying to remember," she said. "It was a long time ago. . . ."

Maria continued to gaze out the window, at the long drop to jagged rocks below. Then she saw a light in the darkness across the gorge. It bobbed like a lantern on the opposite cliffs.

"They're here!" she called to Deirdre. "They must have been marching all the time we were with Cyn." Maria glanced around the room. "Give me the torch," she said. "We can use it to signal them."

Deirdre pulled the torch out of the wall holder. A long stick with oil-soaked rags tied tightly around one end for a wick, it was heavier than it looked.

Maria used both hands to thrust the torch out the window and wave it wildly.

When she pulled the torch back in and gazed out once more, the distant lantern had vanished. Had it been there at all? Then she realized an army wouldn't travel by the light of a single lantern. It must have been an optical illusion of some kind, stray moonlight glinting off a rock crystal. She sighed. "False alarm." She jammed the torch back in its iron holder.

"Now I remember!" Deirdre said. She stood up from the old pallet, brushing grayish straw from her breeches. "Colcorne Gorge was the site of one of largest and most powerful gateways to your world. In fact, I believe that's what started the Trog Wars in the first place."

"What happened?"

"The trogs wanted the gateway for themselves and built this fortress to keep it. The elves and the trogs fought for centuries, and by the time we finally defeated them, when all the trogs were wiped out, this place was so tainted nobody came here anymore. The elves had other gateways to Earth, and just wanted to rest and tell their stories and not be bothered by challenges for a while—but they never *stopped* resting!"

"Do you think that might be what Cyn is trying to do?" Maria asked. "Does he want to find a way to open the trogs' gateway?"

"I wouldn't be surprised."

"But what would that accomplish?"

"I wish I'd paid more attention to what he's been doing with his friends for the last six months!" Deirdre scowled resignedly. "If only we could get out of this room!"

"That doesn't seem likely," Maria said with a sigh of her own. "We're stuck."

"Maria?" a little voice called from outside in the night.

Maria looked up at a pale glow from the window. Friend hovered outside, his little wings fluttering.

"Maria!" the shining dragonfly called excitedly.

"Friend!" she said. "You followed me!"

"Pretty light," he said. "Yes?"

"You saw the torch? Wonderful!"

The dragonfly zipped between the window's iron spikes and fluttered into the room. "Yes, yes, yes!" he called.

"Maybe he can get us out," Deirdre said.

"Shane left the key on the table," Maria said. "If Friend can get it . . ."

"Ask him to try!"

"Friend," Maria said, "come here."

Friend came to rest on her shoulder, buzzing his crinkly transparent wings. "Friend!" he chirped.

"Yes, I'm your friend, and you're mine," Maria told him. "I have something for you to do. It's very important."

"Presents?" Friend asked.

"Deirdre, give me one of your earrings!" Maria said, and the dragonfly cooed and chittered at the glittering white gems Deirdre handed over. "Okay, Friend, here's a present. But I want a special gift in return. You'll have to get it. Understand?" Quickly she explained to him what the key looked like, where to find it, and how to fit it into the lock. She hoped he could lift the key.

"Yes, yes, yes!" Friend said. He flew back out the window and vanished.

Maria rushed over to the door and put her eye to the keyhole. She saw nothing but the corner of the trog table and some of the floorboards from where she stood.

Finally Friend appeared, a glowing light sprawling down the long cold corridors of the keep. The dragon-fly hovered over the table uncertainly, then dipped down out of sight. A moment later he reappeared holding one of the leg bones of the chicken they'd eaten for dinner. Friend struggled with it a moment, then headed for the door.

"No!" Maria called through the keyhole. "That's not the key! It's shiny metal! Do you remember? Shiny hard metal!"

Friend dropped the leg bone and buzzed back to the table. He reappeared with an old rusty nail.

"Key?" he asked.

"Look for a different one," Maria said.

The third time Friend got it right—but the iron key proved heavy for him. He tried to fly up to the keyhole with it, but it dragged him down to the floor instead, where they could see him near the door. He couldn't seem to lift it high enough to insert it into the lock.

"It was a good idea," Deirdre said. "At least we tried."

Then Maria remembered the magic Deirdre had performed during the carriage ride to Metgarde, when she had taken needles and thread and spun them into cloth. That was her talent: She was a spinner, just as Cyn was a mist-mage. Cyn had used his powers to create something much larger, something much more powerful. Perhaps Deirdre could use her talent the same way.

"Deirdre," Maria said, "do you think you could use your spinning talent to get the key into the lock? It's just outside the door."

Deirdre frowned. "I've never tried something like that before. I'd have to be able to see the key."

Maria moved out of the way so the other girl could squint through the keyhole. "I can see it," Deirdre said. She raised both her hands, palms out. "It's moving, spinning very slowly. Here . . . up . . . yes . . . now forward. Yes . . . into the lock . . . spin . . ."

The key scraped with the sound of grinding metal, and then *thunked* to a stop. Maria did not hear the lock click open. Deirdre seemed to be pushing with her mind, squeezing her eyes shut, but the key refused to move farther.

"It's stuck," Deirdre said. "I've turned it all the way, but the lock won't open."

Maria blinked her eyes in surprise. "Try turning it the other way!" she said. "You're on the other side of the door. The key turns the opposite direction from our point of view."

Deirdre laughed at herself. "Of course!"

She concentrated again. The key rattled in the lock, clicked, and turned—but this time it kept turning, and finally with a sound as loud as a shout, the heavy lock clacked open! The door sagged against the jamb.

Deirdre looked surprised and pleased. "I did it!"

When Maria pulled the heavy door open, its ancient hinges shrieked. She and Deirdre exchanged glances.

"I hope Cyn didn't hear that," Maria said.

"Free!" Friend called, swooping down and alighting on Maria's shoulder.

"The gateway is in the lower levels of the keep," Deirdre said, rushing out into the room. "Let's just hope that we don't bump into Cyn in the halls."

Maria agreed. "If that happens, run and trust your luck!"

They hurried along the musty-smelling corridors,

with Friend flying ahead. Each time they passed a window, Maria peered out, but she saw no signs of the king's army yet, nor of Cyn. The moon set, the sky grew darker in the secret hours before dawn. Once or twice, from far above, she heard distant noises: rocks being moved, shouted orders. Cyn and his accomplices would be much too busy to worry about them now.

They trotted down sloping corridors, occasionally clambering down more steep stairways. Each time Maria and Deirdre groaned, but they did their best on the trog-sized stairs to reach the lower levels. Wet, rotten-smelling moss clung to the corners, making their footing slick and treacherous.

Half an hour later, just as the skies began to lighten with coming dawn, they reached an outside courtyard large enough to be a staging area for an entire trog army. The flagstones looked like a dark and rippled sea, broken and heaved upward by hundreds of years of seasonal freezing and thawing. Beyond the flagstones stood a colossal entranceway whose half-rotted wooden doors stood three times as tall as Maria herself. The crude iron hinges resembled lightning bolts scabbed with dark rust. The doors slumped; one had fallen off its hinges and lay at an angle, leaving an opening large enough to pass through.

"Fly away!" Friend called. He fluttered up over their heads, then swooped back. "Fly away!"

"We can't fly," Maria told him.

He made sympathetic sounds and lit again on her shoulder. His long abdomen section drooped. "Poor Maria. Not fly."

On the other side of the courtyard, set against the sheer cliffs on which the fortress hung poised, rose another, smaller tower built into the rock itself. An

ornate metal gate on the bottom glittered with seven
polished locks made of gold and silver. It didn't take
an expert to see that elves had made it rather than
trogs.

The ornate gate stood open, and a dim flickering
spilled into the courtyard. Guard stations made of
blocks of stone stood on either side where trogs must
have been posted at one time.

"That's it," Deirdre said in a hushed voice.

Maria listened, but heard no one moving inside.
Cyn must have been there himself sometime during
the night. He had lit the candles, prepared the gate
for the last part of his plan. Maria wondered when
Cyn would put that plan into action. Sometime this
morning?

Together they hurried to the smaller tower. As they
approached the elven gate, Maria noticed that the
finely crafted gold and silver gleamed from careful
polishing, and the hinges looked well-oiled and
scrubbed free of rust.

"Cyn must have restored it." With her fingertip,
Deirdre traced one of the patterns in the gate. "These
are locking spells. It would have taken him months
to figure them all out."

"Apparently he's very determined," Maria said.

They passed through the gate and into the base of
the tower. Half a dozen candles had been set in beau-
tifully carved holders on the walls. The walls sparkled
as if mica chips had been mixed with alabaster and
then polished to a milky smoothness. A thick wooden
door, carved with designs of interlocking chains, had
been set into the far wall of solid mountain stone.

"This tower is just an enclosure to guard the gate
to your world," Deirdre said in a hushed voice.
"That's it."

A wooden crossbar lay across the door. Large enough to be an entire tree trunk, it rested on top of four large silver hooks in the shape of dragon heads, two bolted into the solid rock and two driven into the wood of the door itself. Strange runes and scribbled designs that looked like hieroglyphics covered the wooden crossbeam.

"Pretty!" Friend said, flitting around in the candlelight.

"Don't move the crossbar," Deirdre warned Maria. "Those are protective wards in the old high elvish language." She took one of the candles from its holder and bent over the runes, straining to read the symbols. "These are very old, and it's hard for me to understand them." She paused. "But some of the root words are clear. . . ."

Maria swallowed. She reached out to touch the door. It tingled faintly beneath her fingertips. "This is a way back home. . . ."

14

A sudden clamor of battle horns and war cries echoed from the gorge below. Using darkness as a cover, the elven king and his army had crept up to the very gates of the cliffside fortress.

The soldiers blew their horns again, and a huge battering ram thudded against the keep's gates. The ground shook underfoot and the sound of hurled boulders shattering on the cliffside reverberated through the air. Dust sifted from the ceiling of the small tower. Friend shrieked and covered his head with insectile arms.

"They must be using catapults!" Deirdre said. "It's an attack, a surprise attack!"

"I thought Cyn was expecting them to lay siege to the keep!" Maria cried. Another catapult missile hit nearby like an explosion. The tower trembled with the impact.

Deirdre nodded vigorously. "He expected our father to follow in the footsteps of the old Trog Wars, just like the legends. Elven warriors would surround a trog camp, then come out at dawn to issue challenges. The battle itself took place around noon, all nice and heroic, so the storytellers could watch and make up their tales afterward."

"It looks like the king is trying a new trick of his own."

Deirdre gasped. "With the army attacking so hard and so fast, Cyn might not be ready with his mist-illusions! What if he's hurt?"

She turned to run out, but Maria grabbed her arm. "They're fighting a battle, Deirdre," she said. "We don't have any armor or weapons. If we go out there and try to help—or even try to stop the army by telling them the truth—we're going to get killed."

The keep shook again as the king's catapults sent missile after missile raining down. A small outbuilding in the courtyard collapsed with a thunderous noise like an avalanche.

Deirdre said. "I can't just leave him out there!"

"From the sound of things, they plan to level the keep," Maria said. "We wouldn't survive ten minutes!"

Battle horns called again. The sounds of shattering stone increased as the decaying ancient keep began to fall apart from the onslaught. Maria heard closer sounds and muffled shouts, then the deadly hammering sound began anew as the battering ram pummeled the enormous gates. The keep wouldn't stand long with only four people trying to hold out against an army.

In fear and confusion, Maria listened to the crescendo of attack. She was angry at the king's wasted effort, angry at Cyn's foolishness, angry at being caught in the middle of it all. She wanted desperately to do something. . . .

The catapulted boulders stopped raining down, but the relentless battering ram continued to thunder against the front gates. The two girls crept to the doorway of the tower and looked across the courtyard. It seemed safe for the moment.

"Can't we help Cyn?" Deirdre said. "And the others?"

"They knew what they were getting into," Maria said. "They started all this."

Deirdre clutched her arm. "There he is! There's my brother!"

Maria followed her gaze. In the dim dawn light, she saw a figure emerging from a half-collapsed doorway in the keep. He held his left arm close to his chest as he staggered across the broken flagstones.

They rushed out to meet him. As they drew near, Maria could see that two arrows stuck out of Cyn's side. His smashed black mask hung askew on his head, and his hands dripped with blood—his own blood.

"Cyn!" Deirdre cried.

"Get me . . . to the doorway . . . ," he whispered. His legs went limp, and he fell to his knees. Deirdre pulled the fearsome jagged mask off and threw it aside inside the enclosed room, then touched her brother's hair, whispering comforting words. Maria now saw a third arrow, this one deep in Cyn's back.

Outside, the battering ram smashed against the front gates. They heard the snapping sound of splintering wood.

"Come on," Maria said. "We have to get him to cover."

Crying softly, Deirdre took Cyn's other arm. Together they half carried, half dragged him to the protection of the small tower. It seemed to take forever. Cyn hissed from the pain.

Inside the small candlelit tower, though, he drew

on some inner reserve of strength. Biting his lip, he began to crawl toward the sealed gateway to Earth.

Deirdre blocked his way. "We have to tell the king!" she said. "We'll make them stop fighting. They must have brought healers with them—that's our only hope."

"No!" Cyn said vehemently. He found the strength to shrug off Deirdre's hands. He worked his way to his feet, moving with painful determined steps toward the door with its huge rune seals and spell-engraved crossbar. "This is our—only hope—" he gasped, "—it's the only hope—for the elven race—"

Cyn squeezed his eyes shut, and without hesitation—as if he knew he would lose his nerve if he thought about it too much—he grabbed the closest, deepest arrow in his side. With a wild yell, he tore it from his body.

Deirdre screamed and tried to grab something to stop the sudden rush of blood. She yanked at her sleeve, biting down on the cloth to start a small rip and then tearing off strips for bandages. Cyn slapped her hand away.

"It's too late for me," he said, "but not for you." With his fingers, he grabbed a cupped handful of his own blood and stretched his arm upward. With blood-wet fingertips, he began tracing the ornate sealing spells, moving his finger along the deeply carved runes. He filled each line with sticky blood.

Outside, at the keep's main gates, the battering ram finally broke completely through the locked main entrance of the fortress. Elven soldiers shouted in triumph as they poured into the courtyard. Maria heard the king himself calling at the top of his lungs: "Prepare to die, foul creatures!"

Cyn said in a throaty whisper, "We must open the

doorway now." He drew in a deep, shuddery breath. "Help me!" He began to strain against the wooden crossbar. *"Help me!"*

Maria suddenly realized that Cyn would have a better chance of surviving if they could get him to Earth. If this gateway truly led to her own Philadelphia, she could dash to a pay phone, dial 911, and yell for an ambulance. Paramedics would be there in minutes to rush Cyn to an emergency room.

She ran to help Cyn lift the heavy crossbar. Centuries of neglect had glued it in place, but Maria strained with all her might. Cyn shook with emotion as cold sweat ran down his grayish skin. The effort made scarlet blood flow faster from his deep wounds.

Maria glanced back. Deirdre stared at them, numb with shock. Between her brother's injuries and the king's attack, she had frozen up inside.

"Come on!" Maria shouted. "It's killing Cyn! *Hurry!* If we get the doorway open, we can take him to a doctor in my world!"

Deirdre blinked once, then came to throw her shoulder against the bar. It still didn't budge.

His voice slurred with pain, Cyn's eyes fluttered shut. He began to chant in a strange ancient language. Maria was too frightened to interrupt him.

As he continued his spell, the blood he had smeared into the carved runes ignited with magic fire, blazing out of the crossbar with bright red flames. The fire licked at the wood but did not consume it.

All the candles in the tower room blew out. The enclosed chamber grew cold as ice, but Maria could still see by the deep ruby glow of the runes.

Cyn collapsed, sliding onto the stone floor like a tossed-aside doll. Deirdre screamed again and fell back. Thick mist flooded the room, taking the shape

of a gigantic trog warrior. This trog, though, appeared more solid than ethereal, as if Cyn had somehow stretched beyond the limits of his mist-magic to create reality instead of illusion.

Maria saw that the dark mist actually rose from the blood on the floor, from the open wounds in Cyn's body. It poured out of him like steam from a kettle, shaping, becoming the shadowy trog.

Now the illusory monster planted its feet firmly on the stone floor, gripped the wooden crossbar with both shovel-like hands, and heaved. The beam rattled in the dragon-headed hooks, but it moved, slowly rising. Then finally, as if the trog had gained a sudden burst of strength, it heaved the bar up and away. It smashed against the far wall, splintering the smooth alabaster-and-mica stone. The crossbar hit the floor with a loud crack.

"Wait!" Deirdre shouted. She rushed forward, trying to keep the huge magic doors closed. But the mist trog shrugged her away, and with what seemed to be the last of its strength—the last of Cyn's strength—it thrust the heavy magical doors wide open.

The world inside the chamber exploded with light and sound from both within and without. The blast streamed outward in a torrent that seemed to go on forever. The floor buckled and jumped underfoot as the ground quaked. The shock wave threw Maria against the alabaster wall. She fell to her knees, covering her eyes and head.

When at last the devastating noise stopped, Maria blinked her eyes to look again. An amazing sight met her eyes.

The scarlet mist had vanished into the air. The giant trog had disappeared. The ruby flames from the spell carvings had sputtered out. And the entire stone wall of the keep had been sheared away—as if half the universe had been exchanged for something else.

The magical gateway still stood in its alabaster frame, but the wall around it had vanished, leaving it surrounded by nothing but air . . . and beyond lay another world. Where the stone cliff walls had been, Maria now saw flat desert sands stretching to the horizon. And, far in the distance, beneath a morning sky filled with pink and golden clouds, Maria could see a magnificent city skyline of tall buildings and winking electric lights.

"Pretty!" Friend darted forward, staring at the distant lights, then flew toward them. "Pretty!" The luminous dragonfly dwindled to a small bobbing white light, then vanished entirely.

Cyn propped himself up, using his last strength to get a glimpse of the gateway to Earth that he had torn wide open.

"It's done," he whispered. "Now it will never close again."

15

Deirdre knelt by Cyn, cradling her brother's head in her lap. Tears flowed down her cheeks as she stroked his forehead, propping him up so he could see through to Earth. His wounds were barely seeping blood now, and his skin looked as pale as milk.

Deirdre held his hand. "Your fingers are like ice," she said. "I wish I could warm them."

Maria came closer, bending over him. Cyn's gray eyes flickered open. He looked first at his sister, then over to Maria; he didn't seem to recognize her, then a faint smile tried to form on his blood-flecked lips.

"Are you sorry I brought you here, Maria?" he managed to say. His voice sounded thin and ragged, like tearing paper.

"Oh, Cyn," she said softly. "Of course not. You brought magic to my world. And maybe you saved your own world, too."

Cyn coughed, and blood flecked his lips and chin. His smile flickered, then grew broader as he closed his eyes. "Charlie and Shane and Felix should be here. Hope they're all right."

Deirdre stared down at her brother for a long moment, then shifted her eyes to look at the incredible

Earth skyline that filled the entire horizon where the keep wall had once been.

Her voice breaking, she explained to Maria, "He used all the power of his life not only to open the gate between our worlds, but to rip it wide." Her lips twisted into a bittersweet smile. "We elves are about to come face-to-face with your Earth, Maria. We will be forced to act and react from now on. There's no more hiding from humans, no more sealing Faery off and settling into lifelong lethargy. Our races will come together—whether we want them to or not."

Cyn gave a groaning sigh, "For the good of us all!" He shuddered and finally lay still. The blood stopped flowing from his arrow wounds.

Deirdre wept, cradling Cyn's head in her hands. Maria found warm tears spilling from her dark eyes, but she knew Cyn would not have wanted crying— not in his moment of triumph, when he had accomplished everything he had set out to do.

He had rallied the elves, gotten them to wake up to their *lives* rather than their memories, made them actually willing to fight for something. Then he had opened up a universe of new opportunities so that the elves could never go back to their drowsy old ways.

Footsteps clattered outside on the buckled flagstones of the courtyard. With loud shouts and cries of astonishment, the elven king and several soldiers reached the small tower. They drew their swords, ready to fight, eager to find a real opponent.

The king drew up short when he saw Deirdre and Cyn on the floor. His eyes moved briefly to Maria, then beyond to the huge open gateway to Earth which now filled the entire wall.

The king began to speak, but then his eyes fell on the arrows still sticking from Cyn's body, and the broken, jagged mask lying on the floor. "Mask," the king whispered. "It had to be." He shook his head sadly. "My poor, poor boy."

Maria could see new life in the king's eyes, like a rekindled fire far different from the half-asleep king whose only joy previously had been playing with the funny toys Cyn and Deirdre brought back from their shopping expeditions.

He strode over to Cyn and bent on one armored knee, moving with intense care. Deirdre looked up at him. "It's too late," she said.

The king hung his head. Another troop of elven guards rushed across the courtyard to give their report. The leader of the troop saluted, ruffling the bright green feather in his helmet. He kept his gaze rigidly on the king.

"Sire! We found three human boys up on the battlements. They are all wounded, and I've assigned a healer to them. They should survive. I thought you might want to question them about what has happened here."

The king nodded gravely, then lifted his gaze to stare at the skyscrapers and blinking neon lights on the horizon, on the other side of the doorway to Earth.

Maria stood and swallowed. That city wasn't Philadelphia, but right now she wanted to be home more than anything else. "I'll be the first one through," she said, "but this door will always be here. Cyn locked it open."

The king said haltingly, as if he had difficulty grasping the magnitude of everything that had changed, "If we elves are going to have commerce with your world now, we will need a friend there. We'll need an ambassador to help us understand things. Would you help us meet with the people of your Earth, and set up an exchange, so that people from your world can come to Faery?"

Maria swallowed. The king's opportunity sounded like a wonderful job, something filled with all the excitement she had been looking for. With a trembling voice, she said, "I'd love to."

Maria turned away from him, mustering her courage before she stepped through the doorway back to Earth.

She felt no different as she took the fateful step. It was like passing from one room to another in a house. But suddenly the air smelled different. The night was warmer, and her feet crunched on caked sand.

Around her, clumps of scrubby sagebrush lent the night a spicy smell. Ahead, the lights of the city blazed with a thousand different colors, flickering neon lights like a huge video game out in the desert. She began picking out signs . . . Caesar's . . . Bally's . . . Excalibur.

"Las Vegas," she whispered to herself. She could hardly believe it. Las Vegas was a long way from Philadelphia, but Cyn had told her that time and distance worked differently in their worlds. She wondered what year it would turn out to be.

Maria looked back at the rift into Faery. A tear in the sky, it stretched half a mile to her left and right and several hundred feet into the air. It was very strange to see the desert night end abruptly in rocky cliffs and pine forest—a slice out of Colcorne Gorge.

And it was stranger still to see the ancient keep of the trogs sheared away, with its back wall entirely removed, like an architect's cutaway drawing of a castle.

On the high battlements, elven soldiers stood staring in astonishment through the rift, their weapons hanging loosely at their sides.

The king of the elves stepped through onto Earth, walking side by side with Deirdre. They both winced in fear and anticipation as they crossed the threshold. Maria went forward to take the king's hand, and Deirdre's, pulling them forward.

Later, she supposed there would be police reports, a phone call to her mom, talks with reporters, challenges and accusations from people who wouldn't believe in Faery no matter what they saw with their own eyes.

But that would eventually change: The doorway to Faery had been opened, and it would stay that way. Maria would bridge two worlds, and she would never be the same—nor would Earth.

Like a flare of rapidly moving light, Friend buzzed over her head, circling. "Present?" he asked.

A smile filled her face as a thought came home to her. All the magic she had ever imagined had come to Earth . . . the humans and the elves would have a lot of adjusting to do.